WHISKEY, YOU'RE THE DEVIL

AN ADDISON HOLMES MYSTERY (BOOK 4)

LILIANA HART

DEDICATION

For Scott,

Because you're my hero and my heart.

OTHER BOOKS

The MacKenzies of Montana
Dane: Volume 1
Dane: Volume 2
Thomas: Volume 1
Thomas: Volume 2
Riley: Volume 1
Riley: Volume 2
Cooper: Volume 1
Cooper: Volume 2
A MacKenzie Christmas

MacKenzie Security Series
Cade
Shadows and Silk
Secrets and Satin
Sins and Scarlet Lace
Sizzle
Crave
Trouble Maker
Scorch

Lawmen of Surrender (MacKenzies-1001 Dark Nights)
1001 Dark Nights: Captured in Surrender
1001 Dark Nights: The Promise of Surrender
Sweet Surrender
Dawn of Surrender

The MacKenzie World (read in any order)
Trouble Maker
Bullet Proof
Deep Trouble
Delta Rescue
Desire and Ice
Rush
Spies and Stilettos
Wicked Hot
Hot Witness
Avenged
Never Surrender

JJ Graves Mystery Series
Dirty Little Secrets
A Dirty Shame
Dirty Rotten Scoundrel
Down and Dirty
Dirty Deeds
Dirty Laundry
Dirty Money

Addison Holmes Mystery Series
Whiskey Rebellion
Whiskey Sour

Whiskey For Breakfast
Whiskey, You're The Devil
Whiskey on the Rocks
Whiskey Tango Foxtrot
Whiskey and Gunpowder

The Gravediggers
The Darkest Corner
Gone to Dust
Say No More

Stand Alone Titles
Breath of Fire
Kill Shot
Catch Me If You Can
All About Eve
Paradise Disguised
Island Home
The Witching Hour

Books by Liliana Hart and Scott Silverii
The Harley and Davidson Mystery Series
The Farmer's Slaughter
A Tisket a Casket
I Saw Mommy Killing Santa Claus
Get Your Murder Running
Deceased and Desist

PROLOGUE

Thursday

I'd once heard a woman describe Nick Dempsey as being sexy enough to make her lady parts regenerate even though she'd had a full hysterectomy. I could sympathize. I had all my lady parts intact and every time Nick walked by I felt my ovaries quiver with anticipation. My ovaries had gotten me into a lot of trouble lately.

My name is Addison Holmes and I'm a sexaholic. Not really, but I'd recently made the life-altering decision to move in with Nick, and quickly found out that years of yoga and romance novels couldn't have prepared me for a man with that kind of stamina and dedication to the craft. I was an amateur in comparison.

Despite his spectacular skills, I was starting to seriously rethink my decision to move my clothes into the space he'd cleared for me in his closet. At the moment, I was leaning toward stabbing him in the forehead with a fork.

"I asked you a question," he said. "What the hell is

this?" He held the white plastic stick as if it were a grenade instead of a pregnancy test.

Sweat beaded on his brow despite the fact it was December and the weather in Savannah had finally turned from hot and humid to slightly cool and humid. His white, button-down shirt sat askew on his broad shoulders and his hair was mussed where he'd run his fingers through it. I was only slightly concerned about the bilious pallor of his skin.

My eyes narrowed and I wouldn't have been surprised if steam escaped my ears like the whistle on a steam engine. So maybe he'd been taken a little off guard by finding the test hidden in a paper bag and shoved in the corner of the closet. What the hell was he doing snooping through my stuff anyway?

"Were you going to show me this or were you going to keep it a secret for the next nine months?"

"If I was going to show you, I wouldn't have hidden it in the closet," I yelled. I refrained from rolling my eyes. But just barely.

The green tinge of his face disappeared and red flushed his cheeks. The little vein in his forehead bulged out and I took a step backward. I recognized the look. I was either about to get yelled at or have the best sex of my life. But because of my excellent proficiency in context clues, I was betting it wasn't the latter.

I bit my bottom lip and felt tears well in my eyes. This was not good. No woman wanted to see a reaction like the one Nick currently had when faced with the possibility of bringing children into the world together. My anger was quickly elevating from steam engine mad to nuclear levels, and if I didn't get out of the house, no judge could possibly hold me responsible for what might happen.

"Answer the fucking question," he said, each word slow and distinct. "Are you pregnant?"

I sucked in a deep breath and felt it burn in my lungs. I don't even remember my hand reaching out to grab the little crystal dish on the sofa table that held potpourri. But before I knew it the dish was sailing through the air, red tinged pieces of wood and cinnamon sticks flying in all directions. It hit Nick right in the middle of the forehead with a thunk that made me cringe. His eyes glazed and then rolled into the back of his head before he toppled to the floor.

What can I say? Hormones are a bitch.

CHAPTER ONE

Monday...Three Days Earlier

I'd deny it if anyone ever asked me, but I hated spending Christmas in Savannah. It's not like it was someplace exotic like Aspen or Utah where snow was pristine and white and made everything look like a Christmas card or one of those Budweiser commercials with the horses that made me cry.

Christmas in Savannah wasn't pretty, but I guess it had its own charm. It had gotten cold enough over the weekend for gray clumps of ice to fall lazily from the sky and melt in a pile of slush once they hit the streets. Window displays in the historic part of town featured brightly packaged gifts and an overabundance of garland, but were somewhat diminished in effect since the cars whizzing past kicked up the slush so it splattered like plops of gravy on windows and people alike.

Christmas lights dangled in neat rows from awnings, and I guess the tourists that flocked to the city during the holidays found it quaint and picturesque, but I found it to be a pain in the ass. Especially since I had to park six blocks from the McClean Detective Agency and slog through the slush and shoppers just to get to work. Bah Humbug.

I didn't have a good reason for my holiday humbuggery. It might've had something to do with the fact that for the first time in my life I felt like a boring grownup. I was a day away from taking the P.I. exam and securing a full time position at the McClean Detective Agency. The agency was owned and operated by my best friend, Kate McClean, and I chose to ignore the fact that my employment had started out much the same as a pity fuck. It turns out I wasn't terrible at the job, so I figured it'd be best if I kept at it. Maybe in fifty years I'll even be considered passable.

It's not like I could go back to teaching. Once upon a time I'd taught ninth grade World History at James Madison High School in Whiskey Bayou, Georgia— which just happened to be the same town I'd been born and raised in. But I'd been let go a few months ago because I'd stumbled over the dead body of my principal in the parking lot of a seedy gentleman's club. It wasn't the stumbling over the body that actually got me fired. It was the fact that I'd been dancing inside the seedy gentleman's club to begin with. And I use the term dancing very loosely.

But really, it wasn't just my now-respectable employment that was giving me a case of the Christmas blues. I was in a serious, committed relationship. I lived in a nice house—granted, it wasn't mine, but I did pick out the little hand soaps and towels in the guest bath, so I figured it was at least half mine. I was driving a very tasteful BMW X5 with leather seats that I'd only dripped ice cream on once. It wasn't the sweet little cherry-red Z

I'd once owned along with a gigantic car payment, but it had wheels and got me to where I was going. But it was just another thing that had been paid for and provided by Nick. Or at least Nick's trust fund.

He didn't like to flaunt it, but Nick came from very old Savannah money. His dad was an alcoholic who couldn't keep his pants zipped, his mother could give Queen Elsa from Frozen a few ice queen lessons, and his older brother was following in daddy's footsteps. Needless to say, it wasn't a close-knit family.

I was proud Nick had managed to break from the mold and forge a life of independence for himself without the help of his parents. But lately, it felt a lot like I was forging a life of dependence on Nick.

Back when I lost my teaching job I'd decided to take life by the horns. Between the bouts of panic, hysteria, and crying over having lost my only respectable source of income and being forced to move back home with my mother, I'd told myself that this was my chance to become the new and improved Addison Holmes. I'd find a job and a new place to live. I'd have adventure and fun. And most of all, I'd throw caution to the wind and just be awesome at whatever I decided to do. Because in my head I was always awesome. It was reality that kept intruding on the awesomeness in my head.

I kicked at a pile of gray slush that had accumulated on the side of the street and didn't even care that it mucked up my bright pink galoshes and dampened the hem of my down-lined black coat with a matching pink lining. I'd put the boots and the coat on that morning in hopes that the cheerful color would perk my mood up a bit, but so far it hadn't worked.

I didn't know what was wrong with me. I had

everything a girl could ask for. My mother hadn't called in three whole days, I had spending money from a job I loved in my wallet, and I had a pink Glock to match my boots tucked in my Kate Spade shoulder bag.

I stopped to grab a coffee and blueberry scone, thinking that was exactly what I needed to perk myself up. I'd just turned left on West State Street and was heading toward Telfair Square when I heard the squeal of tires at my back. I turned just in time to see a bright yellow Volkswagen Beetle take the turn on two wheels, scare the hell out of a group of tourists, and barrel straight toward me.

A piece of scone fell out of my mouth and bounced off the top of my galoshes, but I managed to step back on the sidewalk and avoid the spray of slush as the car slammed on its brakes directly in front of me. The door flew open and Rosemarie Valentine stared at me with crazed eyes.

"Get in, Addison. I'm gonna need backup." Her fleshy breasts were heaving out of the vee of her orange and turquoise argyle sweater, and her face was flushed with anger. The blonde cherubic curls that normally framed her face like Farrah Fawcett on steroids frizzed and crackled like she'd rubbed dryer sheets all over them. Or fornicated with Zeus. You can never be sure with Rosemarie.

I must've hesitated too long because her blue eyes lasered into my soul and the voice of a demon came from somewhere deep inside her. "I said GET IN!" she growled.

I jumped a foot in the air and hot coffee splashed onto my hand. I hauled ass inside the car—not an easy thing to do in a full winter coat with a handbag the size of a small suitcase—and I barely got the door closed before she pressed her foot down on the accelerator and took off like a bat out of hell.

"Shit," I breathed out, my heart thudding in my chest. "You made me drop my scone."

"We don't have time for scones this morning. This is serious."

I closed my eyes as she defied every traffic law imaginable to get us out of downtown, and I was grateful I knew most of the cops in the area. Of course, if they really wanted to help me out they'd pull Rosemarie over and get me the hell out of this car, instead of sitting inside their units and staring at me out of big round eyes as we sped by.

"Jesus. Has somebody died?"

"Worse." She reached into the handbag that was stuffed between her arm and the door and pulled out the biggest vibrator I'd ever seen in my life. It was flesh colored and defied the laws of nature. My nose scrunched up in disgust and I pressed against the car door to put more distance between myself and Rosemarie's love substitute.

Up until last month, Rosemarie had been having regular sex with a man named Leroy that she'd met at the Great Dane Kennel Club. Leroy wasn't much to look at unless you were attracted to Weebles that looked like Danny DeVito, but osemarie insisted his talents were confined to the bedroom.

According to Rosemarie, Leroy was a tantric master. He even gave tantric retreats twice a year and invited me and Nick to come out the next time he held one. I didn't know much about tantric sex. Regular sex pretty much wore me out and made me useless, so I couldn't imagine engaging in anything on a higher plane. But Rosemarie said once you've experienced that level of spirituality you can't ever go back to plain vanilla.

Unfortunately, Leroy was currently in traction. Apparently even a master can be felled by Rosemarie. Which meant for the last month Rosemarie was the most sexually starved and desperate woman I'd ever been witness to. And every day sent her a little closer to the point of no return.

Rosemarie hit a pothole the size of a crater and she had to use both hands to grab onto the steering wheel to control the car. The vibrator shot out of her hand and I watched as it arced in slow motion, end over end, to my side of the car. It bounced once off the dashboard and my hands shot up in the air in surrender. I might have screamed. Because the next thing I knew that phallic fleshy beast had changed its trajectory and was headed right for me.

Seconds before it smacked into my forehead, Rosemarie's hand shot out and she grabbed it out of thin air.

"Oh, yeah!" she screamed with enough gravel in her voice to make the WWE proud. Her hand clenched around the vibrator and she pumped her fist in the air. "Did you see that? I'm like a fucking ninja. Yippee-ki-yay, motherfucker."

I would have agreed with anything she said at that point. She'd just saved me from getting slapped in the face with a device with more settings than anything NASA had to offer.

My phone warbled the theme from Dragnet and I didn't have to look at the screen to know it was Nick calling. No doubt the cops had called him as soon as we'd sped by. My mother's call would follow closely behind. Since I'd moved out of Whiskey Bayou her reaction time wasn't quite what it used to be. But it's still pretty damned good. I declined the call and envisioned the throbbing vein at Nick's temple as he stared at the phone.

"Maybe you should explain why we're escaping the city like Bonnie and Clyde," I said as calmly as I could muster. "I've got my P.I. exam tomorrow morning and the physical tomorrow afternoon. I need to be in the office going over things with Kate today."

"I'll have you back in a jiffy. You're going to ace that test. At least the written part. But first I gotta put a cap in a bitch, and you're my wingman."

I narrowed my eyes at her comment about passing the written part. What went unsaid is that I was still pretty much a disaster when it came to the physical fitness portion of my exam. Despite extra help from FBI Agent Matt Savage—my former neighbor and occasional tongue wrestler before Nick decided to commit—I was still struggling.

I was in shape. Don't get me wrong. But there are those who are built for short distances and those who are built for endurance. If I was a synchronized swimmer or one of those gymnasts that twirled ribbons and leaped around a big bouncy mat I'd probably be good to go. But ask me to do fifty sit-ups in a short amount of time and I turn into a big sweaty heffalump who can only manage to make it to the sitting position if someone is dangling a chocolate sundae above my knees.

"I don't think Kate's going to be too happy if I help you put a cap in anyone's ass. You know how she is about the agency's reputation."

"Well, maybe I won't unload my weapon. But I might

karate chop her in the throat. Or kick her in the knees. I wore my steel-toed boots just in case."

I looked down for the first time to see Rosemarie squeezed into corduroy pants in the same orange as her sweater and black combat boots laced almost to her knees.

"A much better option, I'm sure," I said cautiously. "But maybe you could explain this in a little more detail."

"You know Priscilla's Love Shack down off 204?"

I blew out a breath and knew intuitively that nothing good was going to come of this. Whatever this was. My intuition had increased by about 150% since I'd started working for Kate.

"I've passed by it. They've only been in business a couple of months."

"Yep. And let me tell you, that Priscilla's a real piece of work. She made it big as a porn star back in the nineties and used all her money to retire to live a life of luxury."

"So she moved to Savannah to open a sex shop?" I asked.

"It's not Tahiti, but I can understand it. Those porn stars are about the savviest businesswomen on the planet. I saw a documentary once on the Discovery Channel all about it, and they did a whole ten minute segment just on Priscilla Loveshack. That was her porn star name. Clever how she turned it into the name of her shop, isn't it? You gotta admire a woman with those kind of attributes."

"I know the documentary you're talking about. It was fascinating. Especially the part about how they keep their privates looking like a hairless cat. But you've either got to loathe her or admire her. And you just said she was a real piece of work."

"She is. And you've got to expect it from those porno-business types, but this is the South. She can't come from

LA to Savannah and expect to treat her customers the same way she would in California. Everybody knows you're supposed to be rude to your customers out there. I've seen Pretty Woman at least a hundred times."

"So you're going to pop a cap in her ass because she doesn't have Savannah manners?" I shook my head and grabbed onto the dash as Rosemarie took the exit ramp to head to Highway 204. "I think the sexual deprivation has gone straight to your brain."

"Poor Leroy," she said, clucking her tongue. "We were practicing the Row His Boat move for his advanced tantric class, and then all of a sudden he's screaming and crying out for his mother. It took me a minute to realize he was in pain instead of in the throes of climax. You know, that wasn't the first time he called out for his mother. They were very close, rest her soul."

I bit the inside of my cheek and my eyes widened. I always felt at a loss for words whenever I was with Rosemarie, but I'd learned that silence was usually the way to go.

Priscilla's Love Shack was about a mile down the access road off Highway 204. It was sandwiched between a 24/7 gas station and a Hibachi Grill that looked like it would never pass a health inspection.

Rosemarie's yellow Beetle zipped between cars and pulled into the deserted lot. I was guessing primetime sex toy shopping wasn't Monday mornings. She parked in a space in front of the entrance and it took me a minute to realize what wasn't right about the scene. Other than the fact that giant dildos sat in the display windows and each of them wore a different hat so they looked like penis-shaped Village People.

I whistled long and low and leaned forward in my

seat. "Holy cow. Looks like you aren't the only one dissatisfied with the merchandise."

The glass front door was nothing more than a few jagged shards. The rest had shattered on the front sidewalk. I looked over at Rosemarie and noticed her normally rosy complexion was somewhat pale.

"I should probably tell you something before we go inside," she said, her voice trembling.

I sighed. "It's too early for booze, and Dairy Queen isn't open yet. Be gentle, Rosemarie."

"I maybe broke the door when I came to see Priscilla last night." Rosemarie squinched her eyes shut like a child waiting to be scolded.

My mouth dropped open and I looked back and forth between the shattered front door and Rosemarie's forlorn face. Big fat tears rolled down her cheeks and her bottom lip quivered.

"I'm a felon," she cried, her wobbly contralto rising an octave. "What's come over me?" She grabbed hold of my hand and squeezed so tightly I felt the bones rub together. "Do you think the judge will be sympathetic? I'm a woman on the edge. Sexual frustration can make a person crazy. There's got to be some kind of free pass in a court of law for the sexually deprived."

"Why in the world are we back here today if you came last night?" I asked, exasperated. "You don't return to the scene of the crime."

She nodded sagely, taking in my words. "I didn't think about that. I haven't had all those classes like you have." She wiped her fingers beneath her eyes, smearing black mascara, and then she hit the steering wheel with her fists, making me jump in my seat.

"I was just so mad!" she said. "She was so mean. I

mean, it was every high school nightmare come to life. She was perfect and beautiful and she's obviously successful and knows how to invest. My breasts are bigger, but they sure aren't all perky like hers. Those breasts practically defy the laws of gravity. Mine are only good for feeding third world countries or hanging out laundry to dry if you run a rope through my nipple rings."

I paused for a second at that image and filed away the fact that Rosemarie had nipple rings. Then I sighed and patted her on the shoulder. "You can make yours defy the laws of gravity if you pay the right price. She's plastic. You're the real deal."

"Thank you. That's real sweet, but it's hard to remember that when those plump lips are spewing such hateful things. And if she burns the motor out of her handheld device she can just go to the back room and get another instead of flushing a hundred and fifty bucks down the toilet. I'm a teacher! I don't have a high-priced budget. Makes me just want to tie her up and toss her into the swamp for the gators to munch on. Though the plastic can't be good for their digestive systems."

"Wait. A hundred and fifty bucks?" I said. "Holy shit. For a hundred and fifty bucks that sucker had better give you an orgasm and then get up and serve you breakfast in bed."

"It doesn't make breakfast," she said in all seriousness.

I thunked my fist against my forehead. "You can't go vandalizing things every time someone hurts your feelings. People hurt my feelings all the time and I just ignore them."

"That's not true. I remember you putting shrimp in Veronica Wade's new convertible after she put super glue on your oboe reed and told everyone your lips were raw and peeling because you gave Ricky Lee Gherkin a blow job and got herpes. She deserved every one of those shrimp. "

"That was a youthful transgression," I said primly. And then the corner of my mouth twitched because it had been damned funny to see Veronica's reaction once she got inside the car and was covered in shrimp stink. Veronica Wade had been my archenemy for my entire childhood. And then she'd decided she hadn't made my childhood miserable enough so she decided to teach at the same school I worked at and seduce my fiancé the day of my wedding. If I could go back and put more shrimp into her convertible I'd do it in a heartbeat.

"My point is, we're adults now. You've got to get a hold of yourself and get these sexual urges under control. Maybe if you just go in and apologize and offer to pay for the door then she won't press charges."

"You really think so?"

What I really thought was that Rosemarie needed a sex intervention and her own reality show, but that didn't seem like the most supportive thing to say. "I think it's a start. And you'd better do it in a hurry or you're going to be late for school."

Good Lord. I was even starting to sound like a responsible adult. I was getting sick of myself. I wasn't the type of person who blossomed under the restraints of routine. I was a free spirit. Variety and excitement were my middle names. I just needed a little something in my life to take away the humdrum of the rut I was stuck in. Maybe helping out Rosemarie in the middle of a sex crisis was just what the doctor ordered.

"Come on," I said, opening the car door. "Time to pay the piper."

A cold blast of air and diesel fumes hit me in the face, singeing my nose hairs and making my eyes water, but I embraced it. This was Savannah at Christmastime, dammit, and I would be cheerful.

There would be no more humbuggery from Addison Holmes. I was turning over a new leaf. I was going to kick ass on my P.I. written exam and kick a lot less ass on the physical fitness requirements later in the afternoon, but kicking ass was kicking ass and I was going to do it no matter what.

Rosemarie managed to birth herself from the Beetle and as we approached the front of the shop I started to get that little tingling feeling at the back of my neck that told me the smart thing to do would be to get back in the car and get the hell out of Dodge. But Rosemarie squashed any hopes of doing that.

"Looks like someone cut themselves on the glass," she said, pointing to the shards beneath our feet.

"Damn, damn, damn," I muttered beneath my breath. Blood was smeared on the glass in the shape of a shoe print. Even I was experienced enough to know that it was a lot of blood for someone to have just cut themselves passing through. I stared in through the gaping hole of the door and my eyes followed the trail of bloody footprints through the shop.

"Dear God. Please don't let me find a body."

"What's that, Addison?" Rosemarie asked. "You're mumbling. You've really started doing that a lot lately."

I stared at Rosemarie, and whatever she saw on my face was enough to have her lips clamping together to keep her silence. I still had on my gloves so I pulled open the door and stepped inside. Glass crunched beneath my feet and Rosemarie shuffled in behind me.

"Don't step in the blood," I told her.

"Of course not. That's disgusting." She stepped gingerly around the bloody footprints and held her purse in a tight grasp close to her chest. "Good grief, I barely slammed the thing. And I only bashed it with my handbag once. They don't make doors the way they used to. And I didn't mean for anyone to cut themselves. You think they can charge me for assault along with the vandalism?"

"Hello?" I called out. "Is someone here?"

Other than the broken front door, nothing seemed to be out of place. Videos and DVDs lined the wall on the far right, costumes and changing areas were in the back, and about six thousand varieties of dildos and anal beads lined the shelves in the middle of the store. Priscilla sure knew her business.

A display of condoms and lubricants sat along the counter next to the register, and I was briefly distracted by the Rough Rider and tingling gel combo pack on sale for $9.99. And maybe I was stalling because the bloody footprints had to originate from somewhere. As I got to the counter I realized the blood wasn't just on the floor. Droplets spattered across the counter and the register in a wide arc. I swallowed once and put my hand on Rosemarie's arm to keep her from getting any closer.

"Oh, Lord," she whispered. She started to make the sign of the cross and then she must've remembered she was Methodist because she took a step back instead.

I leaned farther over the counter and looked into the open-eyed stare of who I assumed was Priscilla of Priscilla's Love Shack. Her face was no longer pretty. In fact, it was pretty unrecognizable as human.

"Rosemarie?" I said. "Did you forget to tell me anything else important?"

I didn't think Rosemarie was a cold-blooded killer, but she'd been acting stranger than usual and I wasn't the best at picking up vibes from potential killers. I'd also just heard her say she wanted to toss Priscilla to the gators.

She swallowed and then swallowed again, and I hoped she wasn't going to be sick. Cops hated vomit on their crime scenes. Sweat beaded on her upper lip and she nodded once.

I felt the bottom drop out of my stomach. "It's okay," I told her. "You can tell me anything. I'm your friend."

She grasped my hand and squeezed it tightly. "I forgot to turn the Crock-Pot on before I left for school this morning." And then she fainted in a dead heap at my feet and took me down with her.

CHAPTER TWO

THE GOOD NEWS about having a homicide detective for a boyfriend is that I can call him whenever I stumble over a dead body. The sad thing is I've had to do it more than one might think. Crime was rampant in Savannah. And I was a magnet for finding it.

The first responding units showed up about ten minutes after I'd made the call. Nick was about twenty-seconds behind them and he still hadn't managed to find the right words to say. He'd been shaking his head ever since he caught sight of the body, and the little vein in his forehead was bulging.

"Addison..." He'd repeated my name about five times but never managed to get anything else out. I just waited patiently. I knew he'd get where he was going eventually.

Nick was one of those kinds of guys who could stop traffic the minute he walked into a room. He was a couple inches over six feet and movie star handsome. Savannah PD had been using him as the media liaison for several years because the cameras loved him and he had a gift for smoothing out contentious situations—probably due to his wealthy upbringing and having a senator as an uncle.

His hair was black as midnight and he kept it cut short because it had a tendency to curl, and his eyes were the most devastating shade of blue I'd ever seen. His body was whipcord lean and muscled—like a swimmer—and I could attest first hand that he looked amazing without clothes on. He was a damned good cop, and we'd managed to live together for the last couple of months without killing each other, so I took it as a good sign.

I could tell he was really trying to keep hold of his temper, and I grimaced as I overheard one of the other officers refer to me as the girlfriend of death. Nick probably took a lot of flak for associating with me, but I wasn't going to dwell on it overmuch. I had lots of positive qualities too. I could make brownies and pies from scratch, I could outshoot most of the cops on the force, and I was always picked first whenever we played Trivial Pursuit due to my degree in history and weird ability to remember random shit. I had a lot of not-so-great qualities too, but I figured now wasn't the time to mention them.

Nick fisted his hands just above his duty rig and took a couple of deep breaths. Rosemarie stood off to the side with two other officers while she gave her statement. I shook my head when I heard her beg them not to put her in the same jail cell as Big Bertha and that she wanted her prison virginity to remain intact.

I was almost positive Rosemarie didn't cause the dents in Priscilla's face, but I wasn't ready to swear on a stack of bibles yet. She'd been unstable at best since Leroy went into traction.

"They're not going to arrest her, are they?" I asked.

"I don't know," he said, shrugging. "Depends on what

the evidence says and if she can come up with an alibi after the ME rules time of death. But she's going to be busy answering questions for a while, and she'll be advised not to take any trips out of town. It's pretty damning that she admitted to doing damage to the property."

"I'd like to point out that I'm just an innocent bystander." I held my hands up and tried to give my charming southern smile—the one with a lot of teeth and little substance—but Nick wasn't having any of it.

"Now's not a good time to play that card. Did you just hear Ruiz? He called you the girlfriend of death. That's what every cop in the city calls you."

"It could be worse."

"Really? 'Cause I can't think of anything. Especially since you're my girlfriend."

"You could just ignore them," I said, eyes narrowed. "It's not like I'm the girlfriend of leprosy or—" I waved my hands around in the air trying to come up with a worse example and then it came to me. "Or your mother for crying out loud."

Nick's nostrils flared and he looked down at his feet as he tried to get control of his temper. So, probably bringing his mother into it wasn't the best of ideas, but she really was pretty awful. Of course, now I felt awful for bringing her up when I knew she was a sore spot for Nick.

"I'm going to have an officer get your statement and drive you back to the agency. Try not to find any more bodies between now and when I pick you up for dinner tonight. I don't want to talk about this. I want to pretend it never happened."

I was still stuck on the dinner comment when I remembered we were supposed have dinner with my mother, her new husband, and my sister Phoebe. We were eating out, thank God, because my mother could burn water. That didn't stop her from trying, though.

Nick motioned to an officer I'd never met before and he gave me a stern look before heading over to talk to the Medical Examiner who'd just come on scene.

"I'm Officer Locke," my new babysitter said. He couldn't have been more than a year or two over twenty. If he'd shaved a day in his life I'd have been surprised. His hair was sun-bleached blond and his face still had the cherubic softness of youth.

"Addison Holmes," I said, sticking out my hand for him to shake.

"Nice to meet you," he nodded. "So you're the girlfriend of death?"

***

Locke drove me back to the agency and dropped me at the front door, and I thanked him for the ride and also for hitting a drive-thru to get me coffee to replace the one I'd left in Rosemarie's Beetle. My dad had been a cop, so I'd learned early on that you could get cops to do almost anything involving food or beverages if you offered to pay for it. And I'd really needed the extra caffeine to get me through the rest of the day.

The McClean Detective Agency was located on Telfair Square in a beautiful crumbling brick building of dark red that was overrun with ivy. Black shutters framed all of the windows and the front door was painted black. Tasteful gold lettering that read McClean Detective Agency in the corner of the front plate glass window was the only indication of what went on inside the building.

Kate had started out her career in law enforcement a dozen years ago, but it hadn't taken her long to realize she didn't enjoy the red tape and bullshit that went along with the job. So she went out on her own and opened the agency. She had a handful of fulltime agents—mostly retired cops—but she also employed a lot of off-duty cops part-time who were looking to supplement their income. And then there was me. Like I said, I was the equivalent of a pity fuck.

The temperature had dropped at some point between my blueberry scone and finding Priscilla Loveshack with her face bashed in, and I shivered and pulled my coat tighter around me as I made my way up the steps and opened the door. A warm blast of air enveloped me and I sighed in relief.

Kate was all about class and reputation, and the inside of the agency reflected that. There was only a certain income bracket who could afford her services, so the interior of the building made sure they'd feel right at home as soon as they walked through the door. Despite the "old southern money" decorating scheme, she'd also managed to make it feel like a home.

Except for one thing. Lucy Kim sat in the foyer behind a massive U-shaped desk. She was the gatekeeper and personal dragon for anyone wanting to purchase Kate's services. She did all the initial background checks on the people hiring us, did the billing, kept the office in immaculate shape, and I was pretty sure she fed on the blood of young innocents to keep her youthful glow. I'd tried doing a background check on her once and the only thing that popped up on the page was her name.

Lucy was Asian-American and her hair was so black and shiny you could see your reflection in it if you walked behind her. Her eyes were black, her cheekbones sharp enough to cut glass, and her lips were perpetually red—

probably from her latest feeding. Her stilettos were always sharp and lethal, and I couldn't think of anyone else in the entire state of Georgia who could wear leather pants without the humidity making her thighs stick together. Lucy was just unnatural.

I'd never heard her speak one word in the months I'd been working for Kate, and it had become a personal mission to get something to come from between those lips. For all I knew she was hiding a forked tongue.

"Morning, Lucy," I said, pulling off my winter gear and hanging my coat in the closet. She kept her gaze straight ahead on the computer screen, but I wasn't deterred. Nothing much discouraged me. At least not for long. And then it hit me. A brilliant idea. I got them every now and then.

"You know I was thinking," I said, taking a seat in one of the plush chairs across from her desk. "After my P.I. exams tomorrow it would be fun to have a girls' night out to celebrate. We could go have some margaritas and judge people from an alcoholic haze. It's been forever since we've all gotten together to do something fun."

In truth it had been never. Lucy didn't exactly socialize with her coworkers. Kate assured me that Lucy had a skillset that was extremely valuable in the private eye business, but I had yet to see what it was. I also hadn't managed to get Kate drunk enough to spill the beans, and my curiosity was killing me. Secrets weren't meant for the South.

Lucy took the file folder that was sitting next to her keyboard and handed it to me without ever looking up from the computer screen. I sighed and took it and then sat there a few extra minutes staring at her in uncomfortable silence just to see if she'd look up. She didn't.

"So it's a plan then," I said, getting up from the chair. "No need to bring anything. Just your company is enough. Have a wonderful day."

I remembered my manners and smiled before heading back to the offices. And then I muttered the entire way down the hallway about bad manners and the lack of social skills in some people. I was on a personal mission to break Lucy Kim. I didn't care if I had to spend years devoted to the task. I would get her to speak to me before it was all over.

My office at the agency was a converted janitor's closet. The paint was fresh and the carpet was new, and if I stayed at my desk with the door closed for too long I'd get high from the carpet glue fumes. If I laid down on the floor my head would touch one wall and my feet the other. There was barely room for a small desk, a computer, and a printer, but I'd managed to add my own personal touches anyway, mostly because I had an addiction to Pier 1 and I needed some place to put my animal print fringed floor lamp and red rug since it didn't really fit in with Nick's décor.

My office was at the opposite end of the hall from all the other offices, right next to the bathroom and across from the conference room. I veered in the opposite direction and headed towards Kate's office. She always had coffee and something from the bakery sitting out for potential clients.

I knocked once and stuck my head in the door. "You busy?"

"No. I've just decided to throw the stack of files on my desk in the trashcan and pretend they never existed."

I arched a brow before heading over to the credenza to grab a cinnamon roll and put a pod in the Keurig for a fresh cup of coffee. "I'm going to go out on a limb and guess from the zit on your chin and the snarl on your lips that you have extreme PMS. Here, have a cinnamon roll."

Her eyes narrowed at me, but her gaze cut to the gooey roll in my hand. "I've already had two. It hasn't helped. And I'm buried in cases. I need to hire two more fulltime agents, and Lucy could use an assistant. Business is booming."

"Most people probably wouldn't sound depressed when saying that."

"Well, I've never pretended to be most people. I've been working sixteen-hour days for months. I barely see Mike. Sometimes I roll over in the middle of the night and scare the hell out of myself when I realize someone is sleeping beside me."

Mike was Kate's husband, and he was a cop with the Savannah PD. He worked erratic hours, so combined with Kate's erratic hours I could see how they might have issues spending quality time together.

"I don't even remember what sex feels like," she said, dropping her head down to her desk.

I took a bite of cinnamon roll in sympathy, but mostly to keep my mouth full so I wouldn't say something stupid. I wasn't having any problems remembering what sex felt like. Nick reminded me every chance he got, including in the shower about two hours earlier.

"Look on the bright side. I've got my exam tomorrow and then you can legally add me to the roster."

She brought her head up slowly and her stare was blank and dull. And then she thunked her head back onto the desk. So maybe I wasn't her first choice for new employee additions, but beggars couldn't be choosers. And she'd already promised me the job if I performed at the top of my class, so there was no way I was going to let her take it back.

"So I have some news you might want to hear." I went back to the credenza and got Kate another cinnamon roll and brought it back to set it beside her head. I'd never seen anyone who needed a third cinnamon roll so bad in my life.

"You and Rosemarie found a dead body this morning. I heard it on the scanner when I first came in."

I blew out a breath and gathered up my files, coffee, and cinnamon roll. "Nothing is sacred in this town anymore. I can't even spread my own gossip without someone beating me to the punch."

"Life's a bitch and then you die."

"Have I ever told you how much I enjoy your PMS weeks? It worries me that you're armed." "Not as much as it worries me that you're armed."

"Touché, my friend. You leave me no choice but to get some work done." My exit would've been more dramatic had Kate bothered to raise her head from the desk and see me out. Instead she turned her face to the side and took a bite out of the cinnamon roll without using her hands. I could relate. Sometimes a girl just needed to eat pastries with no hands.

CHAPTER THREE

Most of the cases passed my way were pretty routine for the agency. A lot of adulterers and a lot of fraud. What can I say? Savannah is a hotbed of scumbags and reprobates.

I trudged the six blocks back to where I'd parked my car and sat inside with the heater on full blast while I looked over the file I'd been given. I was grateful for the working heater. I was also glad the car had brakes and didn't have a hole in the passenger side floorboard. I hadn't been so fortunate with my last vehicle.

"Hello," I said, my brows arching in surprise. "What have we got here? Looks like the Enterprise is going down, Spock."

Up until I'd moved in with Nick I'd been renting a small house on a quiet street on the west side of town. The neighbors were nice, the trees were big, and the sidewalks were cracked. Best of all, the rent had been cheap enough that I could almost afford it. If I was being honest, I kind of missed my little house.

My next door neighbor had been Leonard Winkle, or

Spock as he insisted everyone call him. Leonard was a good guy. He spent too much time watching Star Trek reruns and having Lord of the Rings reenactment parties, but below the nerd was a decent guy who I couldn't see veering off the path of the straight and narrow. He'd also saved my life once, so I kind of owed him.

According to the file, Leonard had had a break in about two weeks before and a very rare model of the Enterprise was stolen. It was estimated to be worth just under a hundred and twenty-five thousand dollars.

"Holy shit," I said.

I shook my head at the tragedy of it all. The neighborhood was going to hell in a hand basket, despite the efficiency of the neighborhood watch. The NAD Squad, or Neighbors Against Delinquency, consisted of six of the nosiest people on the entire street. They didn't miss much, which meant whoever broke into Leonard's house knew the weak spots in the neighborhood and how to get around them. It wasn't an easy task. Especially considering the fact that a very capable FBI agent lived on the same street to handle whatever the NAD Squad couldn't.

The problem with having a hundred and twenty-five thousand dollar replica of the Enterprise in your home was that insurance companies didn't really see the value, and their fraud investigator became suspicious when he started digging and noticed Leonard didn't own anything else even close to the value of the Enterprise.

Raymond Free, the fraud agent, was convinced Leonard was trying to collect insurance on a piece that had never been stolen. Leonard's finances were in good shape. He didn't have any debt other than his house, and his job as a computer programmer paid well. That wasn't exactly painting a guilty sign on his forehead, in my opinion. But insurance companies didn't particularly care about justice. They cared about money.

My job was to find the Enterprise and see if Leonard was guilty of insurance fraud. The insurance company seemed to think it was a slam-dunk case. I had my doubts, but I worked for the big guy this time around.

I wrinkled my nose and tossed the file into the passenger seat. My stomach felt kind of squishy and my conscience was having an argument with the practical side of my brain that knew it needed to earn a living. I didn't feel right about ratting on a friend. The best I could do was dig around and see if maybe there'd been a mistake. Maybe Leonard had just forgotten where he'd put the Enterprise.

I put the car in gear and was grateful for the camera in the dashboard that showed the rear view. I wasn't the best parallel parker. But in Savannah that's what you did if you actually wanted to get out and do things. I backed up until the car started beeping a frantic warning that I was getting too close to the car behind me and then I threw it in drive and joined the rest of the traffic.

Gray plops of mush had started to fall from the sky again and I shook my fist at no one in particular. The little old lady driving next to me flipped me the bird and sped ahead, and I sighed in defeat against the heated leather seats.

"Get a grip, Addison. What is wrong with you?" My fingers tightened on the steering wheel. "Snap out of it. Be cheerful. Life is good. You're blessed."

And then for no reason at all I burst into tears. I wasn't a good crier. I always wanted to cry just like Demi Moore in Ghost, where perfectly formed teardrops slid down my cheeks artfully and my eyes and nose didn't get red and puffy.

By the time I reached my old neighborhood I was in full ugly cry mode, so I pulled into the driveway of the house that used to be mine and let it all out. I don't know how long I stayed there with my face buried in the steering wheel, but it was long enough that my nose was completely clogged and I was down to the occasional hiccup.

I took a couple of deep breaths and realized I did feel a little bit better. Maybe it was the stress of so many changes in my life and I just needed to vent a little. I was going to go with that explanation instead of any other likely possibility.

I raised my head and then yelped when I saw a row of faces staring through the windshield at me.

"Holy mother of God," I said, placing my hand over my racing heart. "A girl can't even ugly cry in private. Unbelievable."

It took a minute for the haze to clear from my vision and to realize that I actually knew the people standing there, instead of them being axe murderers waiting for me to get over my crisis so they could chop me up into little pieces.

I threw the car door open and moved to get out but was thrown back by the seatbelt. Mrs. Rodriguez held onto her walker with a two-handed grip and shook her head at me disgustedly. Mrs. Rodriguez had little patience for anything that breathed, so I wasn't surprised.

I jerked against the seatbelt and finally found the latch to unbuckle myself. I slid out of the car with as much grace as someone who couldn't really see or breathe could.

"Jesus," my sister Phoebe muttered under her breath.

"Scary," said Spock.

Byron from down the street nodded. "You look just my granny did after the aliens brought her back. She was never the same after the anal probe."

"Oh, yeah?" I said, narrowing my eyes at them. "You haven't even seen scary yet. Go ahead, suckers. Make my day."

Spock never blinked. I wasn't even sure the man had eyelids. It was one of the creepiest things I'd ever seen on another human being, and I was amazed his eyes didn't pop right out of their sockets every time he sneezed.

I'm not sure how it was possible, but his brown orbs grew at my threat. He reminded me of one of those stress dolls you squeeze until their eyes bug out. Byron, on the other hand, never had much of a reaction to anything. It was hard to see his face at all behind the Duck Dynasty beard and trucker hat he habitually wore.

"I've got brownies just out of the oven and a half-gallon of rocky road," Phoebe said before all hell could break loose.

"Deal." I veered around the group and headed up the stairs that led into the house, not realizing everyone was going to follow behind me.

In all honesty, I was feeling much better after my cry, but with everyone staring at me like that, I needed to save face so I could forget how mortifying my lapse in control was. It also gave me an opportunity to observe Spock in a group setting instead of one on one. It was all part of my master plan to get to the bottom of the whole fraud thing. And I got free brownies and ice cream to boot.

The smell of chocolate wafting from the kitchen almost brought me to my knees and I closed my eyes and inhaled deeply. The pan of brownies sat out on the counter where Phoebe had left them to cool, and they were pure perfection. I sat down on one of the barstools, grabbed the knife next to the tray and cut a big square at the corner. I didn't care about plates or napkins. I was on a mission.

Byron and Spock took the remaining two bar stools and Phoebe and Mrs. Rodriguez stood behind the bar. I'd never actually seen Mrs. Rodriguez sit down. She was probably the oldest person I'd ever met in my life and she barely came up to my chest. She moved at the pace of a turtle and had a mouth like a sailor. And I'd seen her do bodily harm with her walker. Mrs. Rodriguez was nobody to mess with.

I inhaled my brownie and was cutting my second piece when Phoebe set a bowl of ice cream in front of me. I grunted in thanks and dug in.

"Rough day?" she asked.

"Found a body this morning. You'd think I'd be used to it by now."

"Not necessarily," Byron chimed in.

I watched, mesmerized, as brownie crumbs fell into his beard and then disappeared completely, as if the beard ate them. There was no telling what was in there, and I didn't want to know.

"There's lots of factors to consider," he said, grabbing for a second brownie. "Like the method of killing. Sometimes there's more blood and brains with one kind of murder than another, and you might react differently depending on how sensitive you are to seeing it. It's nothing to be ashamed of. We all handle death differently."

I knew he was smiling because his beard moved

upward, but I couldn't see his mouth through the copious amounts of wiry hair.

"I saw a body that had been hacked to pieces with a cleaver one time and I couldn't keep food down for a whole week. You wouldn't believe the mess a little cleaver can make," Byron said.

A piece of brownie dropped out of Spock's mouth and he went a little green. I moved my bowl of ice cream out of the way and scooted my stool to the right just in case he couldn't man up and keep his brownie down.

Mrs. Rodriguez nodded and clicked her false teeth together. "I know what you mean," she said, her accent thick. "My second husband was eaten by big mountain lion, rest his soul." She made the sign of the cross and then immediately spit on the floor. "Jorge was a pussy. Never marry a man who is not stronger than mountain lion." She looked directly at me and then Phoebe, her black eyes small and intense.

"You don't have to worry about me," Phoebe said. "I'm never getting married again. I like my independence."

This was not news to me. Phoebe had been Miss Independent her entire life. She was also Miss Irresponsible and Miss Most Likely to be Arrested, so I didn't worry about it too much, but right now I was a little jealous of Phoebe.

Phoebe was two years older than me and about a million times cooler. She had that natural bohemian flair that only a select few in the world could pull off. We were cut from the same cloth when it came to looks—brown hair and brown eyes, nice olive skin and average body proportions. But there was a little extra oomph added to Phoebe's cloth.

She'd added purple streaks to her hair and she wore a

small hoop in her left nostril. She wore a pair of black yoga pants and a Tiffany concert T-shirt with the singer's image on the front in neon pink. It was ripped and hung off one shoulder, showing the strap of a lime green tank top beneath. I always felt like a buttoned up prude next to Phoebe, but I'd learned over the years you can't change who you really are. Trying to be Phoebe was never a comfortable fit. And it usually got me into trouble. At least, more trouble than I normally managed to get in on my own.

"You are wise," Mrs. Rodriguez said. "Husbands are good for one thing. And most of them are no good at that. They suck the life right out of you and then get eaten by a mountain lion. Did you know mountain lions bite the back of the neck to kill?" She mimicked the motion with her hands and made a cracking sound. "Took Jorge's head clean off. You're much better off being alone with nobody to love."

Spock gagged and put his hand over his mouth and then ran to the bathroom. The rest of us watched him go and then went back to our own food.

"Poor dude," Byron said. "Hasn't been the same since the break in. Jumps at his own shadow."

I perked up at this bit of information. It was just the opening I needed to dig a little deeper. "What break in? What happened?"

Mrs. Rodriguez narrowed her eyes at me and pounded her walker against the floor. "All your fault. You abandoned the NAD Squad for fornication."

I sputtered indignantly. "Wait a minute. Phoebe took

my place in the neighborhood. Why am I getting the blame for Spock's break in?"

"Phoebe is an artist," she said. "How you say? Ahh... creative spirit. She is busy with things simple folk can never understand."

I looked at Phoebe, and the smile on her face was the same one she'd given me when I was nine and got blamed for letting the goldfish die, even though it had been her responsibility to feed it.

I rolled my eyes and pushed my ice cream away. I wasn't feeling so good all of a sudden. And scarfing down ice cream and brownies the day before I had to do the physical fitness test from hell probably wasn't a good idea.

The toilet flushed and Spock came out of the bathroom, a little pale but no longer green. He took his spot on the stool and Phoebe handed him a bottle of water.

"I heard about the break in," I said, patting him on the shoulder. "What happened?"

"It was awful." He turned to face me, his unblinking eyes never wavering from my face. "It happened right in the middle of the day. It was Tuesday, and on Tuesdays they do an all-day Star Trek revival at the SCAD Theater."

Sweat beaded on his upper lip. I stared at his earlobe so I wouldn't get distracted by the no blinking thing and nodded in encouragement.

"I got home at 3:07—a minute later than usual because they had the blinking red lights going at the stoplight on Stephenson—and I knew before I walked through the front door that something wasn't quite right. I've got extraordinary extrasensory skills."

"It's true," Byron said, nodding. "Just like Spiderman."

"Is the time you got home important?" I asked.

"Of course," he said, appalled at my obvious lack of detective skills. "Someone clearly knew my routine. Down to the minute. I know it was that bastard Khan." He looked at me expectantly, as if that should explain it all. And then he sighed in exasperation. Spock was starting to remind me a lot of my mother.

"Khan would've never missed the Star Trek revival unless he was up to something hinky. And I know he wasn't there. When his name was called at roll call he didn't respond with the password."

"Huh," I said for lack of anything better. I'd never actually heard anyone use the word hinky in a sentence other than Velma from Scooby Doo. I wondered briefly if Spock had started doing drugs but immediately dismissed it. He was always like this. Maybe Phoebe could give him a hit of marijuana sometime so he could relax a little.

"Is there another reason you suspect Khan besides his absence from the revival?"

"It's been Khan's goal all along to destroy the Enterprise." Frustration leaked through his normally passive expression and he stood up. "Do you know nothing, woman? He's Khan. KHAN!"

I put my finger to his forehead and pushed him back onto the barstool, and then I narrowed my eyes and leaned into his personal space. "I don't know shit about Khan. But I know I saw a dead body this morning and I'm not opposed to seeing another."

He swallowed once and nodded. "My apologies. I'm overwrought." He took a long sip of water and collected himself and then wiped his face with the bottom of his Avengers T-shirt.

"It's understandable," Byron said. "You've been violated and you don't feel safe in your own home."

Spock looked back at me. "Have I told you I like it when you're feisty? That's why you were so great on the NAD Squad. I knew it from the moment I saw you staring through my window with your binoculars. NAD has a vacancy without you. You're a hard hole to fill."

"Shut up, Phoebe," I said before she could get a word out. She burst into laughter and clapped her hand over her mouth. I knew my sister well, and Spock had left the door wide open with that comment. "Go on, Spock. I want to hear what happened."

He nodded. "Khan came to one of my reenactment parties last month, and he was unable to take his eyes off my Enterprise replica. I keep it on display in a glass case in my dining room. It's the prototype, you know. That's why it's appraised for so much. The very first one ever made, and the basis for all the models that came after it."

His eyes got a dreamy, faraway look in them.

"I won it in a card game when I was at Comic-Con several years ago. George Lucas is terrible at poker."

"What would Khan do with it?" I asked. "Sell it?"

"Oh, no. A true collector would never sell something of that value. He'd put it with his collection and display it proudly. Khan is known for his collection. He practically has a museum in that old house he lives in. Money isn't an object. But neither is stealing to a man like Khan. He's evil. Probably the most vicious and dangerous villain the crew of the Enterprise ever went up against."

I had no idea where fantasy and reality divided, so I just nodded. "Did the police talk to him?"

"Are you kidding me? Khan has every cop and politician in the city in his pocket."

I winced and squirmed in my chair uncomfortably. As someone who'd been raised by a cop and was currently sleeping with a cop, I wasn't too happy to hear that particular insult, and the urge to grab Spock by the throat to shake some sense into him was becoming my top priority, just behind finishing my ice cream. I wasn't going to let it go to waste after all.

I'd just taken a bite when Spock opened his big mouth. "Hey, I know! You can find the Enterprise for me. You're a P.I."

I choked on my ice cream and started shaking my head. "Technically I'm not—"

"You can hunt down that low down, good for nothing Khan and prove that he's the thief he is." Spock scrunched his face up and pounded his fist into his hand, no doubt imagining Khan's face there instead.

"You see, I can't actually—"

"Byron can tell you exactly how to break into his house. He designed the security system."

"It's really a conflict of interest—" I trailed off, the spit in my mouth drying as his words penetrated.

"It's true," Byron said, nodding. "He's got a lot of weaknesses on the property. Cheapskate. I told him he was practically begging for someone to break in."

"Breaking the law isn't really allowed..." I was still shaking my head as the horror of what was transpiring crashed down on me like a bucket of cold water, but I'd lost control somewhere along the way. If I was ever in control to begin with.

"I'll pay you, of course," Spock continued. "What do

you think, Mrs. Rodriguez? Doesn't a ten percent finder's fee seem reasonable?"

"Are you kidding me?" Phoebe piped in. "She's going up against Khan. That's like signing her death warrant. Twenty thousand dollars and not a penny less.

"Umm, hello?" I said, my chest tightening with panic. "Death warrant?" I looked at Phoebe. "You're supposed to be on my side."

"You're right," Spock said, as everyone ignored my protests. "Twenty-thousand is more than fair for the Enterprise. It's only going to appreciate in value. It'll be worth more than five times the current value when my grandchildren are adults."

"You must have the sex to have grandchildren," Mrs. Rodriguez said, her lips pinched together in perpetual disapproval. "I give you those magazines so you can practice, but still you are alone."

She waved her hand in a shooing motion like Spock was a hopeless cause, and I kind of had to agree with her. Unless Lara Croft or Princess Leia set out to seduce him, Spock was likely to remain a virgin for eternity. I got the unholy vision of what it would be like to make love with someone like Spock, eyes bulging and open, staring at you even through the embarrassing parts of sex that everyone knows you're supposed to close your eyes through.

I shuddered and pushed back from the counter. "I've got work to do. Thanks for the ice cream and chocolate. I probably would've committed murder or driven off a bridge if I hadn't had any."

"I hear ya," Phoebe said. "It's best to stay off the road and away from sharp objects on those days."

I had one foot out the door when Spock stopped me. "How are you going to hunt down Khan if you don't gather intel? I thought you'd been taking classes. They're not teaching you very much if you don't know the basics."

"I'll send the security schematics over," Byron said, before the urge to unload my Lady Glock into Spock's unblinking eyes fully registered.

I deliberately took a deep breath and counted to ten. Maybe I needed anger management classes. Or some Xanax. Going from extreme weeping to wanting to commit murder in less than an hour didn't seem healthy. Or maybe I was going crazy like my great aunt Scarlet and would eventually end up sitting naked on my front porch and shooting a potato cannon at passing traffic. Something to look forward to.

"Fine," I agreed. "Give me his real name. I can run a background check at the office. But I make no promises."

"His real name is Dexter Kyle," Spock said. "AKA Khan. The most evil man in existence. Proceed with caution."

"Dexter Kyle, the federal judge?" I asked incredulous. "That Dexter Kyle?"

"It helps that you know him."

I wasn't about to mention that he'd played poker with my dad every Thursday night for the last twenty years.

"Fuck," I said, and slammed the door behind me.

CHAPTER FOUR

I DON'T KNOW how long I drove around aimlessly, but my jeans were making the drive uncomfortable so I unbuttoned them and laid the seat back a little so the sugar in my system could digest properly.

I didn't want to go back to the office. There wasn't anything new to do except study for the written P.I. exam, and I knew all of that information forward and backward. It was implementing that information in real life situations that I seemed to have trouble with.

The other file Lucy had given me was a standard surveillance case. A cheating husband who was about to get his ass handed to him in a divorce if half the allegations the wife had listed in the file were true. I wouldn't be able to start work on that until after dinner. Which begged the question, why didn't more people cheat in the daytime? It seemed to me like there was less chance of being caught, and I'd be able to go to bed before ten.

Nick lived about halfway between Savannah and Whiskey Bayou in a secluded area off the highway. I was just getting used to picking out the little one-lane dirt road hidden by mossy trees, though I still had trouble finding it in the dark. Nick liked his privacy. I liked to pretend I wasn't completely creeped out by the shadows the trees made at night when I looked out the windows.

By the time I drove down the mile of road to the house, the last thing I wanted to see was the yellow Beetle parked in the driveway. My stomach wasn't feeling so good, and I was pretty sure I needed to vomit before dinner.

I parked the car next to the Beetle, but when I looked into the driver's seat Rosemarie was nowhere to be seen. She wasn't sitting on the front porch either, so I grabbed my purse and left the warmth of the car for the drizzling cold.

"Rosemarie," I said, my eyes scanning the area for any sign of her.

Nick's house rose up in the center of the clearing like an oversized piece of origami—smooth white walls and angles at every turn, dominated by floor to ceiling windows in the front and back so you could see straight through. Which I always forgot about until after I'd had my first cup of coffee every morning and remembered I was standing in the middle of the living room in nothing but my underwear. Fortunately, we didn't get a lot of guests.

There wasn't much of a yard, but moss-covered trees hovered creepily, and I was pretty sure they were watching us and would one day kill us and use our bodies as fertilizer so they could take over the world. I'm not sure what brought me to that conclusion, but it seemed as possible as anything else in my life.

I had about an hour before I was supposed to meet my

family for dinner, and it was already starting to get dark. Rosemarie still hadn't made an appearance, and I shivered, wondering if the trees had already gotten her.

"Rosemarie," I hissed out in a whisper. I wasn't sure why I was whispering, but it seemed like an appropriate course of action.

I had my hand beneath my coat and at the small of my back, my palm resting against the butt of my gun, when I heard the rustle of leaves and the snapping of twigs in the distance. All I can say is that it's a good thing I don't have a quick trigger finger.

The leaves rustled again and I saw a flash of blonde peep out from behind one of the trees.

"Addison, is that you?" Rosemarie whispered back.

I let go of my gun and rolled my eyes. "Of course it's me. What in the world are you doing?" And then I looked a little closer. "Are you wearing face paint?"

"Did you come alone?"

"Was I supposed to bring someone with me? Can you come out here? It feels weird talking to the trees. It's like they're listening. And it's creepy."

"Of course they're listening," she said. "If I were you I'd move. These trees are going to eat you one day. Pluck the roof off your house and snatch you right out."

Rosemarie wasn't the most graceful of women and she burst out of the trees like a Chupacabra about to attack its prey. Twigs and leaves stuck out of her hair and she was wearing a green camo jogging suit and bright white sneakers. Mud was smeared across her face and she had a bow and a quiver of arrows strapped to her back.

"I'm sorry, but I didn't get the Hunger Games memo," I said.

"Very funny. But it pays to be prepared."

"For what? The end times? The zombie apocalypse?"

"Here, hold my bow while I look around." She shoved the bow into my hands and whipped out a pair of high-powered binoculars, scanning quickly through the trees and down the road.

"Aren't you cold? Where's your coat?" Rosemarie needed a keeper. I was trying to figure out how I'd been volunteered for the job.

"They had me cornered at the Exxon station downtown. I put my coat on a stack of cans as a diversion and then slipped out the back door. They're wily bastards, but I outsmarted them."

"Wait. Who had you cornered?" I was starting to get a little concerned. This was over the top even by Rosemarie's standards.

"Those rat fink pigs. And I'm sorry, but that includes your boyfriend."

"The cops are following you?"

"Yep. I've spent the whole day at the police station answering questions. They didn't charge me for destruction of property considering my clean record and the fact that the owner of the property is dead as a doornail, but they all had shifty eyes and watched me real close. I know they were peeping through the crack under the door when they let me go to the ladies room. It almost put me off doing my business. Also, the police budget in this city must be awful. That toilet paper wouldn't mop up faerie piss."

I shook my head and closed my eyes for a second, trying to weed out the important information from the not so important. Having a conversation with Rosemarie was like following the little metal ball in a pinball machine as it ricocheted off everything it came into contact with.

"Let's get back to the cops," I said. "Are you sure someone is following you?"

"Do pigeons poop in the park? Of course I'm sure. I've got the senses of a bat."

"I thought bats were blind."

"A common misconception. All their other senses are magnified by about a hundred and fifty percent. Even the sixth sense."

"So what you're saying is you're psychic?"

"I knew you were going to say that," she said, nodding with approval. It was a little hard to take her seriously with her ample mud mask. "I wasn't going to say anything because I don't like to brag, but—"

"Alrighty then," I interrupted. "So you're being followed. What happened when you left the police station?"

"They told me not to leave town and to keep my nose clean. And then they watched me like hawks as I left the building. As soon as I turned the corner I felt the tail. They think I'm just a music teacher, but I've got skills. I watch TV. I know when an unmarked cop car is trailing me."

She had me paranoid by this point, and I hadn't even done anything wrong. I kept looking around at the trees, waiting for the pop of the flash bang just before SWAT burst out of the trees to take us both down.

"So I pulled the old switcheroo on them and drove straight here. I needed a good place to hide out, but I didn't realize you had cannibal trees. Never noticed it before, but once it started getting dark I felt their presence. I'm rethinking my hiding place."

"It's not good to hide from the cops," I said, looking at my phone to check the time. "If it looks like you've got something to hide it'll make them think you're guilty."

"Do you think I'm a killer?" she asked, her lip quivering. "What if I did it and I don't even remember? Like one of those Lifetime movies, where she goes on a killing spree in her sleep and wakes up with blood on her hands. And then she can't remember where it came from."

I knew things were about to go downhill in a hurry. Big, fat tears rolled down Rosemarie's cheeks, leaving a trail through the mud. She was pretty emotional lately. And come to think of it, I was pretty emotional lately too. Maybe I wasn't the best person to talk her down from the ledge. If she caught me in the wrong mood I might try to jump off with her.

"Okay," I said firmly, straightening my shoulders. I decided enough was enough. It was time to get out of this funk that had been plaguing me. And I needed to be there to support Rosemarie in her time of need. "This is what we're going to do."

"I knew you'd have a plan," she said, bouncing slightly in her white sneakers. When Rosemarie bounced her whole body bounced with her. "You always have the best plans. You don't even have to tell me. Remember, I'm psychic. Or at least half-psychic." A frown marred her face. "Sometimes I'm wrong."

"Trying is half the battle." I nodded. "I'm half-Irish and half-English, so that means I'm only half good at drinking and half good at speaking in a fake British accent. And that almost makes me a whole person."

I looked at the time again and realized if I didn't get a move on I'd be late for dinner. And then I realized I hadn't heard from Nick all day. Which wasn't unusual if he was in the middle of a big case, but he usually called to check in and give me an update.

"That's really sweet of you to come to my rescue like that, Addison," Rosemarie said.

I shook myself out of my Nick thoughts and tuned back into Rosemarie. "What?"

"I told you I can read you like a book. It doesn't take a half-psychic to know that you were about to volunteer to find out who the real killer is and clear my name. I just want you to know that I'm here to help in any way possible."

I opened my mouth to speak but closed it again. I knew better.

"Look at me," she said, her face crumpling again. "Is this the face of a woman who will do well in prison? My skin is soft as butter. And Leroy says my natural fragrance reminds him of cotton balls. They'll snatch me up in a red-hot minute and use me in unnatural ways. I've watched both seasons of Orange is the New Black."

"I was going to suggest you come along to dinner with my family, but I guess it won't hurt to see if I can find out any information from Nick about the case. I'm sure you have nothing to worry about. Unless you woke up with blood on your hands this morning and don't remember where you went last night."

"Right," she said, nodding. "Innocent until proven guilty. Where are we eating? I'm starving."

It only worried me a little that she didn't deny waking up with her hands covered in blood. Rosemarie was an enigma.

CHAPTER FIVE

ROSEMARIE MANAGED to get most of the twigs out of her hair and the mud off her face before we headed out to Whiskey Bayou to meet my family. Her yellow Beetle wasn't exactly the best car to go unnoticed in, but I had her drive us anyway, just to see if there was any truth to her suspicions of being followed.

The theme from Dragnet sounded from the bottom of my purse and I dug around until I found my phone.

"Are you seriously cancelling on me?" I said as greeting. My intuition was usually pretty spot on, which is how I managed to do my job so effectively without actually having any real skills.

"I never said anything about cancelling," Nick said. "You know what they say about people who assume."

There was something about Nick's voice—the sexy southern drawl that rasped across my skin and sent tingles straight to my lady parts—and I immediately felt the tension I hadn't realized I'd been carrying around release from my shoulders.

The thing that I'd come to realize about Nick was that

he was my equalizer. I had a tendency to be overemotional and dramatic at times, though I'm a rock during a crisis or lots of blood loss. Nick was steady and had the ability to reel me in without me knowing he was reeling me in. I've been told I'm a handful.

"So?" I asked.

I heard his sigh on the other end of the line and felt bad for giving him a hard time. He sounded tired. "I just caught a bad one. Double homicide and there may be a third victim we haven't found yet. There's too much blood for only two bodies. I won't make it to dinner. Maybe not until next Tuesday. Things aren't pretty."

I grimaced at the thought of how much blood must be at the crime scene and decided maybe I wouldn't eat again until next Tuesday too.

"Not a problem," I said. "Rosemarie is going to pinch hit for you."

"Thank God for the crime in this city. I almost felt guilty for cancelling."

I looked over at Rosemarie to see if she'd heard any of what Nick had said, but she was humming along to Cyndi Lauper and checking her rearview mirror every five seconds. I'd just checked the side mirror myself and saw a nondescript beige Crown Vic merge into traffic from the onramp and settle in a couple of cars behind us.

"You wouldn't happen to know why Rosemarie has a tail, would you?" I asked. There was about three seconds of pregnant pause and that was enough for me to know the answer. And that he was probably going to lie.

"Nope. I have no idea what you're talking about."

"That's what I thought you'd say."

"I don't know when I'll be home. Call me if you need

bail money." He disconnected and I figured that was just as good as saying I love you.

"You think I should try to lose them?" Rosemarie asked.

Her eyes narrowed and her grip tightened on the wheel. The car lurched as her foot pressed a little harder on the gas pedal.

"Or maybe we should just let them follow us," I said. "Maybe they're not following you for the reason you think. Maybe it's a protection detail."

I mentally smacked myself in the head. No one would believe an unmarked Crown Vic was providing a protection detail on a woman who'd been questioned for murder.

"You know, maybe you're right," she said, perking up a little. "Maybe Priscilla's murderer wants to silence me, since I'm probably the last person who saw her alive. I could be in real danger."

"Why would her murderer want to silence you? Did Priscilla say something?"

"Only that she was impressed that I had the vaginal capability to burn out the motor on the merchandise. I do have superior muscle control. I could snap a twig right in two if I set my mind to it."

"Jesus," I muttered under my breath and closed my eyes, trying to clear the mental image from my brain.

We passed the Welcome to Whiskey Bayou—The First Drink's On Us sign and the Crown Vic was still behind us. The great thing about small towns was that any outsiders stuck out like a sore thumb, and if the cop behind the wheel was brave enough to get out of the car, the entire town would know his life story by the time we finished our hamburgers. That was also the bad thing about small towns.

I was born and raised in Whiskey Bayou, just like my mother and her mother. It was one of those places people liked to raise their children and pretend everyone around them was living the American dream. In reality, it was a hotbed of affairs, illegitimate children, and both extreme poverty and wealth—all within a two-mile radius.

It was like living every day of your life under a microscope, only the people watching weren't doctors or scientists, but instead nosy neighbors who could offer no solutions or support, but were happy to spread the gossip anyway and flavor it with their own opinions.

I'm not saying it's true, but it's possible I might hold some resentment toward the citizens of Whiskey Bayou. Let's just say I wouldn't shed a tear if the bayou swallowed it whole one day and it sunk straight to the bottom. After the fiasco that had been my almost wedding and after losing my teaching position, there was nothing short of kidnapping me and locking me in someone's basement that would get me to move back.

We passed the railroad graveyard and a few businesses that had already closed for the evening—because nothing but the Good Luck Café stayed open after six o'clock—and I found a parking spot just in front of the café.

I could see my mom and her husband Vince at a back booth through the plate glass window. Phoebe was already there, and a guy I didn't recognize was sitting beside her. This was not news. Phoebe had paraded a lot of guys through family dinners over the last fifteen years.

The Crown Vic backed into a parking spot across the

street and I rolled my eyes. He wasn't even trying to be subtle.

"Go on in," I told Rosemarie. "I'll be just a minute."

I didn't recognize the plainclothes cop behind the wheel, but by the way his eyes widened as I walked toward him I was willing to bet he recognized me. Nick was well respected at SPD and because of his role as media liaison everyone knew who he was, despite the large size of the department.

He rolled down the window and I got a better look at him. I pegged him for a cop immediately. It was in the eyes. He was somewhere in his mid-forties or early fifties and his skin was sun darkened and sagged just a bit beneath the eyes and jawline. His hair was a light brown sprinkled with gray and his eyes were light brown. He had on a tan polo shirt and jeans. A guy meant to blend in with everyone else.

"What's your name?" I asked him.

"Lester Graham," he said, tipping his head in my direction. "Detective Sergeant." He showed me his badge and I glanced at it briefly. "I told Nick this was a bad idea."

I smiled and watched the tension drain out of Lester's face. I'd found over the years that my smile was my best weapon at disarming any situation, and Lester was just following orders. Nick, on the other hand, was in a whole lot of trouble.

"Why don't you join us for dinner, Lester? Looks like you're out of Twizzlers." There were three empty bags laying on the passenger seat and about forty-two Styrofoam coffee cups tossed onto the floorboard.

He grimaced and looked a little uncomfortable. "That

wouldn't be the best idea. Socializing with a suspect is frowned upon."

"She's seriously a suspect?" I asked. I knew when you lined up the facts that it made sense for Rosemarie to be the prime suspect, but no one paid attention to the facts. It's why the world was going to hell in a hand basket. "Have you spent any time with her? If she's a killer then I'm Jack the Ripper."

"You are the girlfriend of death. Maybe that's not the best comparison."

I snarled before I could control myself and Lester jumped back in the seat. "I am not the girlfriend of death. So I've found a couple of bodies. It's not like I killed them. How about a little sympathy?"

Lester nodded frantically. "And just to be clear, I've never called you that. I've just heard it around. You know how it is with cops."

"Right. Who came up with the name?"

"Jacoby in Homicide," Lester said, throwing Jacoby under the bus to save himself. I nodded and walked back toward the café without saying goodbye.

The little bell above the door jingled and I was immediately smacked in the face with the smell of grilled meat and pine trees. A fat Douglas Fir sat in the corner, listing to one side, covered in ornaments of all shapes and sizes. The wood floor was scarred, the booths were old and the red vinyl seats cracked.

Business wasn't booming on a Monday night, and only a few families occupied booths. They all turned to stare at me as I made my way to the back of the café. I was still a hot topic of conversation in the area, and all the chatter stopped as their eyes bored holes into my back. Then the whispers started with a whoosh, and I knew it wouldn't take very long for the curious to stop by our table on the pretense of asking about my family.

Up until the last year it had always been Phoebe who'd be the most gossiped about Holmes. Phoebe pulled it off with a cheeky smile and a shrug of her shoulders. She didn't care what anyone thought and she did as she damn well pleased. Sometimes I thought she purposefully made the wrong decisions just to live up to everyone else's expectations.

I made it to the table just in time to hear Rosemarie mention Priscilla Loveshack's death and the fact that she was a murder suspect. Rosemarie wasn't the kind of woman who eased into anything gently. Everyone's attention was focused on her camouflaged track suit and animated retelling of how we came across the body.

My mom's new husband Vince looked at me with a raised brow and I gave him a tightlipped smile. Vince had been my dad's captain, and he was retired from the force now. Apparently he'd had a thing for my mom for a lot of years, and I was glad they were both happy. Vince looked like James Brolin and was extremely vocal during sex. I knew this because the walls are incredibly thin at my mom's house.

"They're tailing me as we speak," she said. "You know they've probably got the whole restaurant bugged and are listening to this very conversation."

I took the seat at the end of the table between Rosemarie and Phoebe's date. I didn't need to look at the menu. Anyone who had a lick of sense ordered the half price burgers and dollar beer on Monday nights.

"I don't think Savannah PD has that kind of surveillance budget," Vince said. "I'm sure our conversations are safe."

"At least from Savannah PD," my mom chimed in. "I saw that 60 Minutes special about how the government was monitoring our every move. Big Brother is watching. Gives me the skeevies to know some politician is sitting in his office watching me do naked yoga every Tuesday and Thursday."

My mom was an older version of me—though she'd recently gotten her hair cut in a sleek bob and added blonde highlights. When Phoebe and I were growing up mom had been an accountant and all around superwoman. She'd worn suits and pantyhose during the day, been the homeroom mother, and kept the household running smoothly. She and my dad lived a very conservative lifestyle with a conservative outlook on life.

Since dad's death a few years ago I've had to get to know a whole new Phyllis Holmes. She ditched the suits and pantyhose and started wearing yoga pants and flip-flops. She took paint-by-number classes, played golf badly, and went to naked yoga with a bunch of other fifty plus women. It was like she'd been living a lie her entire life and was just now getting to be herself. She and Vince seemed happy, so I was happy for her. But if I was ever witness to the goings on in their sex life again I'd stick needles in my eyes.

"What's the big deal?" Phoebe asked. "People are seeing you naked anyway. What does it matter if it's other people in the class or old guys wasting our tax dollars by sitting behind their desks with their pants around their ankles?"

"Good Lord, Phoebe," mom said. "What an image. And I'll tell you straight out if any man can get it up watching Gladys Hinkle doing the downward dog buck-ass naked then this country is in bigger trouble than I thought."

Phoebe and I both snickered and Rosemarie gave mom a knuckle bump and said, "Amen, sister." The man sitting to my left wasn't quite so enthusiastic. He cleared his throat and tugged at the knot of his tie.

"I don't know you," I said to Phoebe's date.

"Maxwell Gunter," he said, holding out a well-manicured hand.

"Nice to meet you. How long have you and Phoebe been seeing each other?" What I really wanted to know was when Phoebe had stopped seeing Savage.

I won't lie. Even though I'd picked Nick and we'd decided to have a committed relationship, it still smarted a little to know that my sister had been interested in the man I'd been thinking about sleeping with while Nick and I were broken up. My jealousy made zero sense. But neither did emotions for the most part. And mine made less sense than most people's recently.

FBI Agent Matt Savage was something of an enigma. I hadn't known at the time when I'd moved into the little rent house in Savannah that he lived across the street. It was safe to say his law enforcement skills were somewhat unorthodox. If Nick was a fine wine then Savage was straight up tequila. You knew you'd regret it in the morning, but it was a hell of a good time while you were doing it.

There'd been definite chemistry between us, but I knew he wasn't built for the long haul. He was all flash and no longevity. Did I regret not taking a walk on the wild side with him while I had the chance? Oh, yeah. Was I a little pissed that Phoebe had once again been the one to take the plunge and live dangerously? Most definitely. But life's a bitch and then you die. There was no looking back now. Especially now that Savage had dipped his wick into Phoebe. There were some things sisters didn't share.

Maxwell Gunter looked to be in his mid-thirties and a little buttoned up for Phoebe's taste. She had a tendency to walk on the wild side when it came to life and men. This guy looked like a banker. Or a lawyer. He wore a gray suit, a white shirt, and a boring gray tie. His glasses were horn-rimmed—which, granted, were kind of cute—and his hair was parted and combed neatly on one side.

"Oh, Max and I aren't dating," Phoebe piped in. "Unless you want to give it a go, Max." She winked at Maxwell and I shook my head as his cheeks flushed red and he started to stammer.

"Take it easy, Phoebe. I don't think he's used to women like you."

"Darling, there are no other women like me."

"That's the God's honest truth, sister dear."

"Max came at my request," my mother said. "He sits next to me in my pottery class. He makes the most beautiful fertility sculptures."

"And no doubt you told him about your two daughters," I said under my breath. But mom had always had ears like a hawk.

She smiled at me and I recognized it as the same smile I'd given Detective Graham just a few minutes before—saccharine sweet and up to no good.

"Max is a dear friend of mine, Addison Holmes, and last time I checked I was allowed to invite friends to dinner without an ulterior motive. And where is Nick tonight?"

She glanced down at my hand and saw there was still

no ring on my finger. Nick and I were living in sin for all the world to see, but to my mother that wasn't making a commitment. Really, to anyone south of Atlanta that wasn't a commitment. In the South, commitment meant standing up in a church in front of two hundred of your closest friends. Nick and I weren't there yet.

"He caught a double."

Vince winced and signaled the waitress to come take our orders. Once she'd left us alone again Vince said, "I heard about it on the way here. It's a bad one. You might not see him for days."

"So he tells me." I shrugged. "I'm used to it."

There were a lot of wives and girlfriends of cops who couldn't take the long and erratic hours and the high risk of the job. I'd been raised as if it were normal since my dad's days on the force, so to me the most irritating thing was that Nick always took the seat facing the door when we ate out and he always slept on the side of the bed closest to the door.

"Max is one of the top defense attorneys in the state," mom said. "Isn't that right, Max?"

It was then I realized what she was doing. Mom had kind of adopted Rosemarie—like a stray puppy or one of those children you sponsor from another country. Mom would've heard the reports as soon as we'd found the body and notified the police this morning. She had a scanner in her car, so she knew the juiciest bits of gossip to pass around at all her hippie classes.

"I'm very good at my job," he assured her. "I understand you ladies had an exciting morning."

Rosemarie was buttering a roll and not paying any attention to Maxwell. I figure she'd written him off as an unacceptable substitute for her burned out motor, and after thinking about what she'd said about her muscle control and snapping sticks in two I was hoping she'd give good old Max a wide berth, so as not to put another man in traction.

I nudged her beneath the table and she looked up, a startled expression on her face and butter greasing her lips.

"Maxwell is a defense attorney," I repeated for Rosemarie's benefit.

"It's like all the stars have aligned in my favor. Because I'm pretty sure I'm going to need some defending." And then Rosemarie burst into tears and tore off toward the kitchen, knocking her chair over as she fled.

I heard a couple of bangs and shouts and winced as a stream of swear words floated out the swinging door.

"It's been a difficult day for her," I told Maxwell. "But in all honesty, she could probably use the help just in case something goes wrong."

"That's why I'm here." Maxwell winced as pots clanged and Rosemarie started swearing back at the cook. "She seems a little unstable."

"She's just had a rough month. She broke her tantric master and it set her on the path to destruction."

"Understandable. I was in traction for almost six months after an unfortunate tantric incident."

Phoebe perked up at that and scooted her chair a little closer to Maxwell's. "I had no idea sex could be so dangerous."

"Oh, good grief, Phoebe. Stop raping the man with your eyes. He's here to save Rosemarie," Mom said.

"He looks like a capable multitasker."

"I swear, Phoebe, your father and I did not raise you to talk that way at the dinner table. If you're going to make your move do it in the backseat of the car like everyone else in this town. If I had a nickel for every child conceived in the backseat of a car in Whiskey Bayou I'd be a rich woman." Having said her piece, Mom refilled her beer from the pitcher.

"I've busted up my fair share," Vince said. "It sure made my nights on patrol a lot more interesting."

Mom nodded and had to talk a little louder because World War III was happening in the kitchen. "I'm pretty sure you and Phoebe were both conceived that way. And let me tell you, that was a task. Your father didn't like to experiment outside the bedroom."

Everyone in the café had turned their attention from the kitchen to stare at my mother as she let out that little nugget of information.

"Jesus, mom," Phoebe said.

My smile was tightlipped. I loved my mother dearly, but sometimes I missed the buttoned-up accountant. "I love family dinner night." Maxwell hadn't moved a muscle and I figured for a defense attorney to be caught off guard—especially after some of the things he'd heard over the course of his career—wasn't such a shining endorsement for my family.

"If you think this is bad, you should see what Thanksgiving is like."

The thought rightfully horrified him and he sucked down a big gulp of his beer. I sat back in my seat and decided it was best to focus on Rosemarie and what was going on in the kitchen instead of thinking of my father—who was not a small man—knocking up my mother in the back seat of his squad car.

"You remember Daphne Dreyer," mom went on. "She was just a few years behind you in school, though Lord knows she's never amounted to a plugged nickel. Her mama's always beside herself wondering what to do with that girl. Just a couple of months ago Daphne got caught down off Route 1 at the edge of the bayou in the backseat of an old Camaro."

"Ooh," Phoebe said, shaking her head. "Amateur move. Camaros don't have near the backseat room as the classics."

Mom arched a brow at Phoebe and Phoebe grinned back sassily.

"Anyway, it turns out Daphne's foot kept pressing against the horn on the steering wheel and one of the deputies was riding by with his window down when he heard it. By the time he got there he said that car was rocking so hard he was surprised the tires still had air in them. And there was Daphne and little Duane Johnson going at it like rabbits, their legs hanging out of the open window and him wearing nothing but his socks."

"The socks are the most awkward part of sex," I piped in. "There's no sexy way to take off your socks. You either leave them on or you both have to stop and get out of the moment to peel them off."

"It's because they cover the feet," Phoebe said. "Feet aren't sexy to most people. But I bet if Nick had a foot fetish, taking off your socks would be the best foreplay of your life. Socks are like a bra for the foot to a foot fetishist."

"I never thought about it that way."

"I always tackle the difficult discussion topics," Phoebe said wisely.

Vince had been part of the family long enough to know to keep his focus on the burger he was putting into his mouth.

"My point is," mom said, veering the conversation back in her direction, "that Daphne is twenty-seven years old and Duane is nineteen."

"Good for her," Phoebe murmured under her breath.

"And there she is, old enough to know better, but getting caught bare-ass naked in the back of a Camaro with a boy that doesn't have the sense that God gave a turnip, because now Daphne's pregnant. And who's going to take care of that baby? It's not going to be Daphne, bless her heart. She works better on her back than on her feet. And it's not going to be Duane either. He still hasn't graduated from high school. Which leaves her poor mama the one left holding the baby."

"It's a damned shame," Vince opined. "But in my experience the one thing dumb people are good at is breeding. It turns out sex is something everybody can do."

"And praise Jesus for that," Phoebe said. "Because how boring would life be otherwise."

Another crash came from the kitchen along with a whoosh that had the hair standing up on the back of my neck.

"I think I need to go check on Rosemarie. Things don't sound so good."

"Damn, I was just about to volunteer to do that," Phoebe said.

"You snooze, you lose." I pushed back my chair and headed toward the chaos. Just as I pushed open the swinging door Rosemarie came barreling toward me, followed by a cloud of black smoke that burned my eyes and lungs.

"Look at my kitchen!" A short, bony man dressed in torn jeans and stained white t-shirt emerged from the smoke. He had a meat cleaver in his hand, and I remembered what Byron said about how much damage a cleaver could do to the human body.

"What the hell?" I yelled as Rosemarie knocked me to the ground in her attempt to escape. The swinging door smacked me in the side of the head, and I got to my hands and knees and managed to stick my hand out before it smacked me a second time.

"Come on, woman," Rosemarie yelled back at me. "This is no time to dillydally. The whole place is going to burn to the ground."

With that announcement, everyone seated in the restaurant hauled ass and pushed and shoved their way out the front door. Rosemarie hadn't been kidding. The kitchen was in a shambles and flames whooshed up from the grill almost to the ceiling.

Someone picked me up from under my armpits and I looked back, a little dazed. The door had whacked me pretty good and I was seeing stars. Or maybe it was just the smoke. Vince's face appeared in my vision.

"It's probably a good time to leave. If I wanted a burned hamburger I'd have stayed home and let your mother cook."

I burst out into laughter and let him help me outside. I could see why he and my mom got along well together. It took a good sense of the absurd to love a Holmes girl.

CHAPTER SIX

Tuesday

There are two kinds of people in the world—those who can function in the mornings and those who can't. I fell into the first category, and I've been told on more than one occasion that it's an annoying trait to possess.

Nick fell into the second category. Though there was one part of his body that woke up alert and ready to go every morning. It was currently poking me in the back and didn't seem to have any intention of going back to sleep.

"What time did you get home?" I asked. It was just shy of six in the morning, and though I woke early and alert, I also slept like the dead and hadn't felt him get into bed.

"About half an hour ago." He snuggled in closer behind me and his hand cupped my breast.

"Long enough to recharge, it feels like."

He laughed, low and raspy, and kissed the side of my neck. Nick was really good at a lot of things. But he was exceptional at sex. Like All-American exceptional. If sex was a sport he would've lettered many times over. He was so good at sex that he gave me the illusion that I was pretty good at it too. And that took an amazing amount of skill. Because once I orgasmed I was pretty much the man in the relationship and wanted nothing more than to roll over and go to sleep. Unfortunately, Nick usually had at least another half hour of stamina at that point and he oftentimes required me to be conscious for it.

"Recharged doesn't even begin to describe it. And I figure I owe you one for missing dinner last night."

He rolled me to my back and parted my legs with his knee, sliding smoothly between them. My pulse was beating about a hundred miles a minute and things were starting to tingle in all the right places.

"I'm thinking you owe me two or three for missing dinner. I wasn't sure I'd ever get the smoke out of my hair."

"I hate to tell you this, babe, but you didn't. Though now that you mention it, I'm getting hungry for a hamburger."

He sniffed at my hair and then bit my neck hard. I huffed out a breath and pushed against his shoulder, but he chose that moment to slide deep inside of me and my eyes rolled to the back of my head. Twenty minutes later I was just about to see God when Nick froze.

"Don't stop! Are you crazy?" My nails dug into his back and I used my yoga-trained muscles to wrap my legs higher and tighter around his waist. I could tell by the hitch in his breath that he was as close as I was, but still, something had made him stop.

"I swear to God, Nick, I'm about this close to doing violence if you leave me hanging here."

"I heard a noise downstairs."

"I don't care if it's the Russian mafia tap dancing on your kitchen counters. I'm about to come." I squeezed my vaginal muscles tight and he groaned with pleasure. "And so are you."

"Race you to the finish line."

He'd just started to move again when I heard the noise this time, and I froze beneath him. I could've sworn I heard the blender going. Or maybe a chainsaw. It was hard to tell with the blood rushing in my ears like it was.

"I don't even care that someone's in my house right now. I'm that close. At least I'll die happy."

"It's just Rosemarie. She spent the night in the guest room. Ohmigod! Right there. Do that again."

Nick froze again and I screamed out in frustration, grabbing one of the pillows and smacking myself in the face with it to muffle the sound.

"Rosemarie is in the guest bedroom?"

"Can we not talk about this in another thirty-five seconds? Preferably after we've both come? For cripes sake."

"Addison—"

"Fine. Your negotiating skills are top notch. I'll make it twenty seconds."

I threw my weight sideways so we rolled and reversed positions and I was on top. I wasn't even going to make it twenty seconds, and by Nick's swiftly indrawn breath I was guessing he wouldn't either.

"Twenty seconds," he said between clenched teeth. "Better get to work." His fingers dug into my hips and I started to move. I loved a challenge.

I'm not sure how we ended up on the floor. Apparently a lot can happen in twenty seconds. The sheets were tangled in our legs and there was a broken lamp a few feet away. It didn't matter. I was paralyzed from the neck down. Like I said, Nick was excellent at sex.

"A murder suspect is sleeping in my guest bedroom?" he asked once his heart rate reduced to a normal speed.

I tried lifting my head to look at him, but I didn't have the strength so I dropped it back down to his shoulder. "Don't be such a hard-ass. It's just Rosemarie. You know her. She wouldn't hurt a fly."

"Baby, her prints were all over the murder weapon we found at the scene. They're going to arrest her today."

"Ohmigod." My head jerked up at that and I caught Nick in the chin. I rubbed at the top of my head while he rubbed at his chin and said, "That's impossible. There's no way she killed that woman using that kind of violence. I took her to the range once and we drew faces on watermelons before we shot at them. She dry heaved for five minutes after I blew away the first one."

"You shot watermelons at the range? I can't believe they let you do that. They're usually pretty strict."

"Only at the civilian range. Bunch of pansies. I shoot at the cop range."

"Civilians can't shoot at the cop range without an escort. Who takes you?"

"Are you kidding? I don't need an escort. Denny Brice and my dad were best friends. His wife threw my wedding shower." Denny was retired from PD now, but he worked at the range to supplement his pension.

Nick quirked a brow and shifted beneath me. "Did you get to keep all the gifts even though you didn't get married?"

"Nope. Had to return each and every one, along with a note. Except for the KitchenAid mixer Greg's mother gave me. I kept that. Figured she owed me one for birthing a son that was such an asshole."

Nick's chest vibrated with laughter and he pulled me in closer. "If it makes you feel better, I agree with you about Rosemarie. She doesn't have what it takes, and things at the crime scene don't add up. But they've got to follow the facts and do it by the book."

"I thought you were in charge."

"I'm not impartial. They handed it over to Jacoby."

Something nudged at my subconscious, but considering I could barely remember my name I didn't try too hard to bring it to the surface.

"It's just as well anyway, because my plate's full with the case I caught last night. It was a bad one." He stretched and then pulled at the tangled covers. "Speaking of, I need to get back to work. How did we end up on the floor?"

"The Lord works in mysterious way."

"I did see a white light toward the end there."

I snickered and untangled myself from his hold. "Watch out for the glass. I don't want to spend the morning picking shards out of your ass."

"That lamp was an heirloom. Belonged to my great-grandmother."

"Oh, geez. I'm sorry." I had visions of trying to glue the shards back together in hopes of saving a piece of Nick's family history, but more than likely I'd end up gluing my hands together.

"Don't be sorry. My great-grandmother makes my mother look like Betty Crocker."

"Wow. You have a hell of a family."

"I like to pretend I was adopted."

"Sometimes I like to pretend that too. Especially after

the time I went to hot yoga with my mother. There are some mother-daughter moments that should never be shared."

Nick used the sheet to scoop up all the broken glass and rolled it up in a ball. He was a typical male when it came to housekeeping, which wasn't surprising since he had a cleaning lady come in three days a week and do it all for him.

I winced as he left the balled up sheet in the corner and made a mental note to take the whole thing out to the dumpster. All we needed was for Rhonda to pick it up while she was cleaning and cut her arms off.

I still wasn't quite used to having a cleaning lady. It felt weird for someone else to handle my underwear, much less wash our sex sheets or remove a pair of handcuffs Nick had accidentally left attached to the headboard. I'd seen Rhonda three days a week for the last couple of months and I still wasn't able to make eye contact.

"I'm going to get in the shower. I'll pay you a hundred dollars if you can get Rosemarie out of the house before I come downstairs."

"You paid me five hundred when you needed me to meet your mother."

"Rosemarie isn't in the same league as my mother."

"That's the truth." I grabbed a pair of boxer shorts and a T-shirt from the drawer and pulled my hair back in a ponytail. I normally liked to shower with Nick in the mornings, but it looked like he was going solo today. "But don't keep thinking you can throw money at me to do your dirty work. You've still got the rich boy mentality that money will solve all your problems."

"Sweetheart, it certainly makes them easier."

It was kind of hard to argue with that.

An hour later, I'd showered and changed into black yoga pants, a purple sports bra, and a black hooded athletic shirt. I laced up my purple Nike cross trainers because I've always felt that if a person is going to sweat then they should match while doing it.

I put on my black baseball hat and stared at myself in the mirror. I gave my reflection a couple of determined looks and flexed my muscles once before grabbing my shoulder bag and heading downstairs. I was going to kick ass today. I'd ace the written part of the P.I. exam and I'd score in the top percentile of the class during the physical part.

My agreement with Kate was that I'd place near the top in all portions of the test to get my license. I'd placed first in the conceal to carry class. Not a problem, since my dad had raised both Phoebe and me to be comfortable around guns. I outshot most of the cops on the force. The written exam would be a piece of cake. I was a history major, for cripes sake. I knew how to study, and if I read it my brain would remember it forever. It's one of those skills that made me valuable for things like Jeopardy and Trivial Pursuit.

I decided what I needed was a pep talk. "You got this, Addison. You're going to shred the records on the one-mile run. And you're going to do it without throwing up." My stomach felt a little queasy at the thought of going straight from the run to the push-ups. "And you're going to make those push-ups your bitch!"

I growled just for good measure and moved my feet like a boxer, giving a practice left jab or two as I made my way to the car. "And then you're going to do some chin-ups and you're not going to cry because it feels like your arms are falling off."

I revved the engine and threw the SUV in reverse, plugging in my iPod as I sped down the driveway. I punched up some Metallica and blasted it as loud as my eardrums could stand. By the time I got to the end of the driveway I remembered that I was old and loud music hurt my ears now, so I turned it down to a respectable volume and scrolled down my playlist until I found Kings of Leon.

My stomach was still roiling with nerves, but I pushed ahead through my pep talk. I needed all the help I could get. "And then it's the sit-ups."

I took a deep breath and did something I hadn't done in a long while. Not since my fiancé had left me at the altar. I'd been a little angry at God for the past year.

"Dear Lord," I said, biting my bottom lip. "I know I've been absent lately. If you want to know the truth, I'm a little pissed at you." I winced and scrunched up my nose. "Sorry. Not pissed. You can't say pissed to God. I'm just saying I've had kind of a rough year, though things have evened out here toward the end. I've kind of got a job and I'm having good sex. Sorry again. You probably don't care about the sex thing. Though thanks for that. I'm pretty sure Nick has ruined me for all other men.

"Good grief, you've gotten me off the subject. What I'm trying to say is that I need a favor. I freaking hate sit-ups. Am I allowed to say freaking?" I handled the wheel with one hand and dug around in my purse for some gum. All this talk was making my mouth dry.

"Listen, I don't know what it is about them, but I've got some kind of mental hang-up. Mostly because it feels like my intestines are being rearranged and I almost always have to pee about halfway through. Also, they're just hard, Lord. In what kind of world do we live in where sit-ups are a natural part of life?"

My stomach was doing major flips now as I turned onto Montgomery and headed toward the police academy where the testing was taking place. "It's not like I'm going to go to the supermarket and everyone there is doing sit-ups to fight for the last roll of toilet paper."

A crash of thunder came from nowhere and I jumped in my seat. The skies opened and a mix of slush and rain came down heavily. The weathermen liked to call it thundersleet.

The dreary grayness of the morning was depressing, and I took this as a sign that a.) I'd been talking too long and God wanted me to wrap it up, b.) I really wasn't supposed to say freaking or c.) He wanted me to get to the point.

"What I'm asking for is a little help. I need this job with Kate. So if you could see fit to make my abs a little more spectacular than usual and get me to the end in record time then I would appreciate it. Oh, and also please let Rosemarie not be a murderer. Amen."

A spot opened up right in the front row and I took that as a sign that God was taking my request under consideration. My stomach still felt queasy, but I was hopeful things would go in my favor.

CHAPTER SEVEN

By noon I'd realized maybe God was just as pissed at me as I was with him. There'd been a perfectly reasonable explanation for the roiling in my stomach. I had cramps like a motherfucker, and if one more person told me how pale I was I was going to stab them in the throat with my #2 pencil. No wonder my moods had been so volatile.

It had taken me about an hour and a half of the allotted four hours to take the written exam, so I laid my head down on the desk and took a nap, intermittently mewling like a cat as the cramps got stronger.

I knew I was in trouble when we broke for lunch. I could barely stand without doubling over, and I knew there was no way I could do the physical fitness portion of the test unless there was a miracle. I had an hour and a half for either my uterus to fall out so I could throw it off a bridge, or for drugs to kick in. The problem was I didn't have any drugs with me. And they'd made me check in my gun at security, so that option was out too.

I had plenty of time to make a quick stop. I didn't care

about lunch. I'd probably throw it up anyway. What I needed was some heavy duty painkiller.

I sped through the streets of Savannah with purpose. The rain had let up some, but was still a soaking drizzle, and the entire city looked to be covered with gloom and dreariness. Or it could've just been the cramps talking. I dialed Phoebe just before I got to her street.

"I'm about to pull into your driveway. I need drugs," I said when she answered with a "Yo."

"Cramps?"

"Fuckin' A."

"Doctor Phoebe will fix you right up. I've got the good stuff."

Those were the best words I'd heard all day. Well, maybe the second best words. Nick had whispered some pretty good ones while he was busy knocking my internal organs loose.

Phoebe was waiting for me with a glass of wine and two white pills when I pulled into the driveway. I'd never been so glad to see Tylenol in my life. I eyed the wine closely, the responsible side of my subconscious whispering that drinking alcohol before a grueling physical fitness exam was probably a bad idea.

The other side of my subconscious looked a lot like Ryan Gosling. And Ryan could talk me into almost anything. Right now he was looking into my soul with his beautiful blue eyes and saying, "Hey, girl. Take the wine. Drink it. You know how much I love you when you drink. And I know how much you love me when you drink too."

"Hello," Phoebe said. "Earth to Addison."

I took the wine and the pills and knocked them straight back. "Sorry, I was talking to Ryan Gosling."

"Sometimes I talk to Channing Tatum. He always

gives me excellent advice."

"Really? Because he seems like a bit of a loose cannon."

"He's much more responsible now that he's become a dad. I hardly ever end up naked in awkward situations anymore. You want something to eat to soak up the wine?"

"Might as well. But I'll have to take it to go. And probably I shouldn't eat anything that's going to make me throw up."

"A good rule to live by in general," Phoebe said, shaking her head. "Sucks you have cramps on test day. I used to use that excuse for real back in high school."

"I remember." I rolled my eyes. "You're the only person I've ever known who gets her period 143 days a year."

"That's the best thing about having men for teachers. They don't keep track and they don't want to talk about it. A girl having her period can get away with murder."

"I'll make sure to pass that along to Rosemarie if they throw the book at her." I took the sandwich Phoebe made me and thanked her again for the painkillers. I was already able to walk upright and it no longer felt like ice picks were being stabbed into my back.

By the time I made it back to the police academy I had so much energy my scalp was sizzling with the electrical force of it. I called Phoebe after I'd checked in and waited for the others to get ready to start the mile run.

"What the hell did you give me?" I hissed into the phone. "I only wanted some Tylenol."

"And that's what I gave you. Along with a Xanax. You sounded a little high-strung when you called and I figured you just needed to chill out."

"You can't just give people drugs without warning them first."

"If I'd told you then you wouldn't have taken it. Look how much better you feel now."

"You know meds always have the opposite effect on me. Me taking a Xanax is like taking speed. Jesus, Phoebes."

"Oh, I'd forgotten that you had that problem. I kept thinking it was Aunt Scarlet."

"Grrr," I said into the phone and smacked myself in the forehead. The guy next to me gave me a funny look and moved over to whisper to another guy, so I gave them both my best PMS look.

Leave it to Phoebe to pull one of her stunts and then casually blow it off. I hung up, knowing it was a futile battle to argue with her. She'd never acknowledge that she did anything wrong. To her it had been the right thing to do, and that's all she cared about. I loved my sister, but she was the most selfish person I'd ever met in my life. And her entire life people had been making excuses for her because that's what "creative" people did.

I tossed my phone into my bag and stretched a little. I was feeling pretty good. And if I ignored the fact that my hands were jittery and I couldn't stand still, then I could almost forget that I wanted to murder Phoebe.

Three hours later I was drenched with sweat and my arms and legs felt like noodles. But I'd finished. And I hadn't vomited once. The medicinal high was wearing off very quickly, and I knew it wouldn't be long before I crashed hard.

I shuffled to the front of the building and barely had the strength to hold my purse on my shoulder. It took me three tries to take my gun from the security checkpoint and drop it in my bag. All I wanted in life was a big glass of wine and Nick's Whirlpool tub.

What I didn't expect was Savage to be waiting for me at the bottom of the steps. I had a split second to decide whether to turn around and run back inside or meet him at the bottom. Judging by the grin he gave me, he knew exactly the battle I was struggling with.

"Long time no see, stranger," he said.

The spit in my mouth dried up and I'd never been so glad to get my period in my whole life. Except that time when I thought I might be pregnant—I'd been pretty glad to get my period then too.

"You could say that." It looked like running back inside was out of the question. I'd opened my big dumb mouth and now I was stuck.

Savage leaned against the door of his truck and I casually looked him over. He looked good. Really good. And the lady driving past must have thought so too because she swerved and almost hit a park bench when she caught sight of him.

He wore jeans and black boots and a black shirt that showed every ridged muscle in his abdomen. His black leather jacket hid his gun and a black ski cap was pulled over his hair. He sure as hell didn't look like law enforcement of any kind, much less FBI. He never quite managed to dress to regulation—Savage didn't like rules. His skin was the color of copper and his cheekbones flat and high, showing his Native American heritage. If the Rock and Pocahontas had had a love child, it would've looked like Savage.

He was a renegade, sexy as hell, and the kind of man mothers warned their daughters about. Which meant he was just about irresistible. But somehow I'd managed. I'm such a dumbass sometimes.

"You're looking a little worse for wear, babe."

I shot him the finger and he chuckled. "You're lucky I'm too weak to pick up my gun or I'd shoot out your tires."

"If you did that I couldn't take you to get celebratory ice cream."

I perked up at that. Now that the physical fitness exam from hell was over I could eat as much ice cream as I wanted. Not that I'd been curbing my appetite much before the exam, but I'd at least thought about it.

"What are we celebrating?"

"Your new job. You came out number 4 overall. Good job, babe. I knew you'd conquer those sit-ups eventually."

I clamped my mouth shut and didn't tell him the only reason I'd done so well was because Phoebe drugged me. I didn't know what the status of their relationship was, and honestly, I didn't want to know. But I also didn't want to cause them any problems.

When Savage had said it had been a long time, he hadn't been kidding. The last time I'd seen him was the week after I'd moved in with Nick. Savage had kept his word and continued to help me train and get into shape, but I couldn't look at him without thinking about what might be happening with Phoebe, and me living with Nick made things a little awkward. Or probably it was just me. I had the ability to make almost any situation awkward.

"Are you sure? Results aren't supposed to be posted until Friday."

He arched a brow and then opened the passenger side door of his truck and waited for me to get in. "Of course

I'm sure. I've got connections. And they all owe me favors."

"That's handy."

I made my way down the stairs, trying not to wince as my hamstrings tightened up. Savage's truck was on and the heater was running, and when I finally managed to hoist myself up into the seat I let out a very unladylike groan. My phone rang as soon as Savage took his place behind the wheel and I wondered if Nick had some sort of sixth sense when it came to Savage.

"Hello," I answered.

"So how'd it go?" Nick asked.

"Pretty well, despite the fact that Phoebe gave me a glass of wine and a Xanax for lunch."

There was silence on the end for a few seconds and then Nick said, "I'd ask you if you're kidding, but I know you're not. I just wanted to call and tell you congratulations and let you know you placed fourth overall."

"Yeah, I know. Isn't it great? I'm employed!"

"How do you know? Results aren't released until Friday."

"Umm—" My gaze cut to Savage and I saw his lips twitch in amusement. Nothing much got by him. "Savage told me."

There was more silence on Nick's end of the line. "I didn't realize he was back from the task force."

"Yep," I said, since I hadn't realized Savage had been gone on a task force job to begin with.

I decided the best thing to do was to change the subject before things spiraled downhill. Nick was not a fan of Savage. Mostly because he knew Savage had been trying to get me naked for the past few months. Savage was mostly ambivalent toward Nick, but I think it was because he knew it irritated Nick. Sometimes I thought there was a little too much Alpha male in my life.

"So will you be home for dinner?"

Nick sighed, recognizing the tactic for what it was. "Doesn't look like it. Try to stay out of trouble. And don't take any more drugs from Phoebe."

"Now you tell me," I said and disconnected.

Savage drove through Dairy Queen and I got a hot fudge sundae with extra fudge—because I believed in celebrating the right way—and Savage got a strawberry shortcake sundae, which brought down his Alpha status only slightly in my estimation. But I wasn't going to judge. At least not out loud.

"You're judging me," he said as soon as I had the thought.

"It doesn't count if it's silent. Everybody knows that. Besides, you have to expect it after ordering strawberry shortcake. Fruit will always be inferior to chocolate."

"Maybe if you ate more fruit instead of chocolate you'd be able to walk downstairs without whimpering right now."

"Hmmph," I said and scooped up a glop of hot fudge in my spoon. "Nick said you were on a task force."

"Just got back yesterday. We had a series of murders across multiple states. Ended up all the way in Virginia. I'm glad to be back in my own bed."

"Phoebe didn't tell me you were gone." There. I'd done it. I'd brought up the elephant in the room. And was pretty damn subtle about it, if I said so myself.

"I'm not sure I mentioned it to her. I let Spock know so they could keep an eye on the house."

"Oh." I chewed on my bottom lip and wondered what

to say next. "I just thought the two of you might have— you know—communicated."

"Not after our initial hellos and an occasional nod as neighbors. She wasn't you, babe. She was never even in the running."

"Oh, man." That was not what I had been expecting him to say. No one had the ability to complicate my life more than Savage. "I have cramps," I said, just for good measure.

The corners of his mouth twitched but he kept his gaze straight ahead. "I'll keep it in mind. It's always good to know one's obstacles when going into battle."

"Are we having a battle?" Nerves skittered down my spine and I got a funny feeling in the pit of my stomach. I loved Nick. I knew in the bottom of my heart that he was the right choice. But that didn't mean the temptation wasn't there when Savage was in the picture. And the harder he pressed, the more I struggled with the temptation.

"Love is a battlefield, sweetheart."

"Seriously? A Pat Benatar reference and strawberry shortcake?"

"I'm comfortable with my masculinity."

"I'm in a relationship with Nick."

"I've heard the rumors. That doesn't mean we can't be friends though, right?"

I narrowed my eyes and stared at him intently, trying to figure out what his game was. "You want to be friends? Just friends?"

His grin was slow and deliberate—I was a sucker for his smiles—and my nipples hardened like pebbles as my lady bits started humming.

"Just friends is always a good start, don't you think?"

"Listen, Savage—"

"I've got two weeks of vacation since I've been working overtime the last two months," he interrupted. "I hate vacation. I like working. Why do they make you sit at home and pretend like that's fun?"

"Maybe you should go to the beach or something."

"Want to come with me?" He waggled his eyebrows then added, "Just as friends, of course."

"No, thank you," I said primly. "I'm overloaded with cases at the moment."

Lord, I was such an idiot. Why couldn't I be a vixen and always know exactly what to say when men flirted with me? Bat my eyelashes and play coy. Give them a saucy wink and a half smile that held no promises. Instead my face was like a TV screen, broadcasting every thought that flitted through my brain so all the men in my life could see I was a giant boob when it came to having any kind of game whatsoever. I'd convinced myself over the years it was an endearing trait instead of pathetic.

"Perfect. I can help you with your cases and not die of boredom the next couple of weeks. What do you have?"

"Umm—" I hadn't seen that one coming. Savage was excellent at throwing the occasional curveball, and Nick was going to commit murder if the two of us worked together again. Savage and I in close quarters was never good, mostly because his tongue almost always ended up knocking my tonsils around and sometimes my hands strayed into dangerous territory. "I'm sure there's nothing that would interest you. It's petty stuff, really. Routine."

"If it keeps me from hosting the neighborhood watch meeting at my house this week then sign me up. What can I help you with?"

I thought about it for a second and realized I probably

could use Savage's help. Nick wasn't exactly forthcoming when it came to gathering information, and Savage didn't mind breaking the occasional rule. I had a feeling when it came to Khan I was going to need someone who didn't mind getting their hands a little dirty.

"What do you know about Dexter Kyle?" I asked.

And just like that, the playful grin that had been on Savage's face turned into a hard line and his expression closed down. "I can help you with anything but that," he said. "Toss that case in the trash and run far away. What else do you have on your plate?"

"Wait a minute? Are you serious? I can't just toss it away. People are counting on me."

"I can't believe Kate would take on a case involving Dexter Kyle. She knows better. Where's the paperwork?"

I chewed on my bottom lip, trying to figure out what I was missing. I'd known Dexter Kyle my entire childhood, and I'd even called him Uncle Dex. My dad had never had anything but a good word to say about the man, and now all of a sudden everyone got weird whenever his name was mentioned. Granted, it had been fifteen years since I'd really seen the man, and I'd obviously had no idea he had such a hard-on for Star Trek paraphernalia, which just goes to show you don't really know what goes on in anyone's private lives. Now I had to decide just how much to tell Savage about the favor I was doing for Leonard Winkle to get his Enterprise back.

"Silence from you is never a good thing. Tell me what's up, Jessica Fletcher, and what kind of trouble you've gotten yourself into."

"You know, a little faith would be nice every now and again. I don't know why you'd automatically assume that I'm in trouble." I turned in the seat to give him what for and the muscles in my legs seized up. I whimpered in pain and rubbed at the knotted muscles. "This is all your fault."

"I'm pretty sure it's your lack of water intake and need for salty foods that's at fault, but I'm willing to shoulder part of the blame."

If I'd had the ability to do bodily harm at that moment I'd have taken the opportunity, but I couldn't spare the energy to do anything more than bare my teeth at him. We were stopped at a traffic light and he leaned over the seat and started massaging my aching muscles, and I whimpered in relief as they unknotted bit by bit. And then once I could think again I realized that Savage had his hands on me and no good could possibly come of that.

"The light's green," I said, glancing over to find his dark eyes watching me closely.

"I know."

"I'm with Nick. And you're poaching."

"I know that too." He gave my leg one last squeeze and then put the car in gear and started to drive. "I understand why you picked Nick. I'm not the safe choice. And as chaotic and wheels off as your life is, you crave that safety. It's one spot in your life where things are normal and how they're supposed to be. But I've got news for you, babe. You're never going to be satisfied with normal."

"Your psych minor is showing." My back was stiff with indignation and a little hurt that he thought I'd never have a normal life. Or be normal, for that matter. "And for your information I love Nick very much."

He smiled that infuriating grin but stayed silent. I didn't know what any of it meant, but I had a feeling I might be in trouble.

CHAPTER EIGHT

"DON'T THINK I've forgotten how this all started," Savage said. "How are you involved with Dexter Kyle?"

I sighed and decided the best thing to do was table anything that involved hormones for the foreseeable future. Maybe God really was looking out for me after my earlier conversation with Him. Maybe He'd sent the cramps to save me from myself. It was as good of an explanation as any.

"It doesn't really have anything to do with me. It has to do with Spock. Apparently his house was broken into a few weeks back and someone took the Enterprise."

"Ahh," Savage said, nodding. "Now I get the connection."

"Really? That's all the information you needed to get it?"

"It makes sense Khan would want the Enterprise for himself. Either that or destroy it altogether. It fits the pattern."

"For crying out loud," I said, shaking my head. "It's

like a secret club or something. I had no idea the scope of the Trekkie world."

Savage arched an incredulous brow. "Did you grow up in a cardboard box or something? How was your childhood so lacking?"

I held out my hands in surrender. "My apologies. I grew up on Blossom and Growing Pains. I was learning about the important stuff that happens in the teenage years. It's no wonder Spock is still a virgin."

"No worries, sweetheart. I'm not. Just in case that's what's holding you back."

He turned his gaze in my direction and his eyes went soft and black with desire. I felt the rush from the top of my head all the way to the tips of my toes, and I realized it was probably a good thing I'd never ended up doing the horizontal mambo with Savage. I probably would've blacked out from the endorphin rush before I got the chance to see if the area below his waist was as exceptional as the rest of him.

"Maybe you should drop me off at the corner," I said, my hand feeling for the door handle. I was ready to jump out and roll into the street if need be. I had not been prepared to see Savage or to have these feelings come back. I'd spent the past two months adjusting to the thought that he was sleeping with my sister. And now that I knew that wasn't true my brain and emotions didn't know how to adapt.

"Chicken."

"Oh, yeah. I can only handle so much excitement in one day and my ovaries are winning that race."

"That's a lovely mental image. I knew there was a reason I missed you. So what's your involvement in

Spock's break-in?" he asked, shifting the topic back around to his original question.

I explained about how the insurance company had hired the agency to prove that Spock was committing fraud and how I'd somehow gotten talked into proving Khan was guilty of the theft.

Savage let out a low whistle and said, "Kate is going to flip her shit if she finds out you're working for the accused party."

"I figured this might be one of those 'need to know' kind of cases. And since you offered I could use the help."

"I actually didn't offer. I believe I told you to stay away from Dexter Kyle."

"Oh. That's disappointing. My plate is kind of full what with Rosemarie being accused of murder."

"Hello," he said, brows raised almost to his hairline. "You forgot to mention that one."

"You should've stayed with the task force and your serial killer. Things are pretty crazy around here."

He pulled the car into the parking lot on the side of the police academy. My SUV sat alone in the back of the lot."

"Okay, I've got a plan."

Just hearing him say that made me feel about a million times better. I could almost be competent when I worked with Savage. Though every time I worked with Savage I usually ended up in more trouble than I started with. He was a magnet for trouble.

"I could get in serious trouble for this, because the information is classified, but I want you to be aware. God knows you won't listen if I tell you to stay away from him."

"Hey! I listen," I said indignantly. "Sometimes."

"Uh-huh. Kyle has been under investigation for almost five years for ethics violations. He's a smart guy, and it's been hell to pin him down. We've had undercover agents who've been in place on his staff for the past couple of years, and it's not going to be long before major shit goes down. You don't want to be caught in those crosshairs. Believe me."

I felt like I was having an out of body experience. "Are you sure? I've known this man since I was born. He was one of my dad's oldest friends. He brought me a porcelain doll back from Austria, for cripes sake."

"Oh, well if that's the case, I'll tell them to call off the investigation."

I rolled my eyes at his sarcasm. I don't know why I always found that trait so attractive in men. Unless they were using it on me—then it wasn't so attractive anymore. "Very funny. I just can't see the man I knew as someone who could be guilty of those things."

"People do bad shit for a lot of reasons," Savage said, shrugging. "And there's a big difference as to how you thought of him as a child versus how you'd see him now. You said that you haven't seen him in years. People change."

Something in his voice had me looking at him a little closer. His expression was guarded and his focus intent on the road. And then he grinned and the moment was over.

"Let me do some digging around tonight. I'll pick you up at the office in the morning and fill you in."

I felt like something had shifted during our time in the car together, but I wasn't sure what or how it would affect us in the future. I gave my sundae a sad glance and wished I'd thought to get a second, and then I hefted my bag and got out of the truck.

Savage waited until I got into my car before he drove away, and I started it up and put it in reverse. My phone rang and I put the car back in park, wondering what else could possibly happen today. I wasn't sure how much more I could fit in before I decided to go back to Phoebe's and ask for more drugs.

One day I'm going to learn to stop asking what else can happen. I didn't recognize the number on the caller ID, but it was a local area code so I answered.

"Hello?"

I could barely hear the person on the other end of the line. "Addison, it's me. Rosemarie."

"Why are you whispering?"

"Because I don't want Detective Jacoby to overhear our conversation. He took my emergency pack of M&Ms out of my purse. Can you believe the gall of that man? Just snatched em' right out and now he's eating them out in the hallway. I was saving them for the zombie apocalypse. I saw that tip on Doomsday Preppers. It's always important to keep a snack on you at all times in case the zombies invade and you're nowhere near your go pack. It'll sustain you until you make it to your stash."

"Rosemarie, I'm confused. Is Savannah being invaded by zombies?" My head was starting to pound and I rubbed the spot between my eyes.

"Not that I've heard, but they don't have a TV at the jail, so I'm not up on my current events."

My stomach flipped and I banged my head against the steering wheel once before resting it there. Nick's words came back to me from that morning, and I wondered how I could be such a selfish friend. All I'd been worrying about all day was my P.I. exam, my sister's bad judgment, cramps, and Savage's irresistible pull. I'd forgotten all about Rosemarie.

"Addison—" Her voice was weak and tear-filled. "I'm a convict! They put me in handcuffs right in front of my neighbors and everyone." Her voice hitched. "I'll never be able to show my face in Whiskey Bayou again. You know how it is. I'll lose my job. I'm like the second reincarnation of you. I'll be an outcast."

"Hey, it's not that bad. You'll still be able to show your face in Whiskey Bayou. You'll just have to get used to everyone whispering about you once you decide to show it."

"Who's going to take care of my dogs while I'm in the hoosegow? They'll become a ward of the state."

"I'll take care of your dogs. Don't worry about that. What we need to worry about is getting you out of jail as quickly as possible. Have they set bail?"

"There's supposed to be a hearing in the morning. I don't think I'm cut out for this." Hysteria was starting to tinge her voice and I couldn't say I blamed her one bit. I'm not sure what I would've done in a similar situation. "The sheets on the bed hurt. I'm delicate. I break out in hives if the wrong kind of fabric touches my skin. And there's only one toilet. And it's right there in front of everyone. What kind of respectable southern lady does her business right there for everyone to see?"

"I can't think of one," I said automatically and then wished I'd kept my mouth shut. But really, people in the south didn't even talk about going to the bathroom in polite company, much less consider letting anyone watch them doing it. Nick and I had been involved, off and on, for months, but our bathroom business was private.

"What am I gonna do?" she wailed.

"I want you to call Maxwell Gunter as soon as you hang up. He'll be able to tell you exactly what needs to happen. Mom said he's a great attorney."

"And he's single too," she said.

"A very important piece of information to have as far as him keeping you out of prison is concerned."

"Would you mind calling him for me? I used my one phone call to call you. I knew you'd know just what to do."

"Thank you, Rosemarie. I'm touched." And I was. I'd never been anyone's first choice to be their one call from jail before. "What did Jacoby say when he arrested you? What were the charges?"

"Second degree murder, and he said if I confessed they'd reduce the charges to manslaughter. He said they had me red-handed and a jury would lock me up and throw away the key."

I was hating Detective Jacoby more and more with each passing day, and not only because he'd been the one to coin me the girlfriend of death. I'd never met the man and couldn't have picked him out in a lineup, but he seemed like a real asshole. I was totally fine with making judgments like this with no basis in fact. I was a pretty good asshole detector.

"What evidence do they have?" I knew they'd found her prints on the murder weapon from what Nick had told me, but Rosemarie might have more information.

"He said my prints were all over the fire extinguisher that bashed her face in."

"Why would your fingerprints be on the fire extinguisher?"

"Because she dropped her cigarette into the trashcan

and the whole thing burst into flames. Apparently a bottle of lube had broken open and she'd tossed it into the trash. It makes you wonder what's in that lube to make it catch fire like that. You'd think it'd peel the skin right of your lady parts with that kind of fire- starting power."

I pounded my head against the steering wheel at the image that thought provoked.

"Okay," I finally said. "That's kind of bad luck. Were anyone else's prints there besides yours?"

"I don't know. They're not real forthcoming with information. If Jacoby wasn't such a dickwad he'd be kind of cute. He reminds me of Eric Estrada. Except white and balding. But otherwise he's the spitting image."

"Huh..." I said.

"Listen, I've got to go. Jacoby is pointing at his watch. Lord, I really want to do that man bodily harm. Next time he steals my M&Ms he'd best watch out. I'm not above a little police brutality. It's not like I've got anything left to lose."

"Before you decide to go Full Metal Jacket on anyone let's just step back and take a deep breath. I'm going to call Maxwell for you, and then I'll go by your house and make sure Baby and Johnny Castle are all taken care of," I said, referring to her Great Danes.

"You'll need to give Johnny Castle his meds. They're in the refrigerator. Thanks again for taking care of everything. You're the best. And I have confidence that you'll get this all figured out so I can be set free. "

I was still stuck on the fact that I was going to have to give medicine to a hundred and sixty pound dog, so I didn't really clue in on the fact that she was putting her faith in me to figure out who really killed Priscilla

Loveshack. All of a sudden the phone disconnected and I was left with a whole new set of problems.

It didn't take long to contact Maxwell and fill him in on everything that was going on, though quite honestly I was surprised he took my phone call at all after the family dinner the night before. He must've been made of stronger stuff than I'd originally thought.

I was also thinking he didn't have much of a sense of self-preservation considering he ended the call by asking me out to dinner. I told him he'd be better off asking out Phoebe, considering she was the one who wasn't currently living with another man, but Max said that Phoebe scared him a little. I could understand how she'd have that impression on a man, so I didn't press the issue.

I passed the exit for Nick's house and groaned a little in defeat. I was sweaty, dirty, and wanted to sink into the jetted tub and possibly sleep for a full twelve hours. Instead I was driving into Whiskey Bayou so I could get eaten by two dogs that were the size of small horses. Baby and Johnny Castle were nobody to mess with, and I hoped to God they remembered me.

Rosemarie lived not too far away from my mom's house in one of the newer subdivisions. All the houses were one-story and small, lined up side by side like Legos, with small porches, bricked mailboxes, and a single tree planted in the front that wouldn't get big for another thirty years. The blue house smack in the middle of the street belonged to Rosemarie.

I parked in the driveway and left the car running so I wouldn't have to warm it up again, and I checked my appearance in the rearview mirror before I got out. I looked like I'd been through the wringer. Dark circles under the eyes. My complexion pale and a little clammy.

And I was pretty sure I was getting a zit on my forehead. Stupid hormones.

Dusk had already come and gone and it was pitch black as I got out of the car. None of the neighbors were out in this kind of weather, which was nice considering I didn't particularly want to have to talk to anyone looking like I did.

I trudged around to the backyard and released the latch on the gate, slipping in as quietly as possible. All I needed was for one of the neighbors to be looking out the window and report "suspicious activity."

It was a postage-stamp-sized backyard and the dogs had pretty much destroyed any chance of grass growing. Rosemarie kept an extra key under an empty flower pot and I let myself in the back door, flicking on the lights as soon as I walked in.

The house was in disarray from where I assumed the cops had gone through looking for anything that would help them gather evidence—bloody clothes or shoes that matched the prints taken from the scene.

I heard whining from somewhere in one of the back rooms and wiped my damp palms on my yoga pants. It was now or never. Hopefully they'd kill me quick if they were going to do it, instead of letting me linger for several days while snacking on my corpse. Okay, so maybe that wasn't the most positive of images to have flitting through my brain, but those dogs terrified me.

Rosemarie treated them like overgrown babies. I'd once seen her full out kiss Johnny Castle right on the lips, and she had no problem with the tongue or the slobber that was generated by that beast. It wasn't natural, but Rosemarie didn't have any living relatives in the area anymore, so I wasn't going to pass judgment.

I looked in the refrigerator and found the medication and then made my way down the hallway to the last room, where the sounds of whimpering and clawing at the door came from.

"Poor puppies," I said through the door. "It's gonna be okay. Mama had to go to jail for a little while, but Auntie Addison is going to take good care of you."

I put my hand on the knob, but my hands were sweating so badly that I had trouble turning it.

"Please don't eat me," I said and pushed the door open. Baby and Johnny Castle both sat a few feet away, their tails wagging furiously, curious expressions on their faces. When Baby had been hit by a car a couple of months back I'd helped Rosemarie take care of her and get her to the vet. I was hoping she remembered that I helped save her life.

I had no idea what I was going to do with them, but I knew they couldn't stay here alone. Already they'd eaten a pillow and feathers were all over the room.

"Hello there," I said tentatively. "Do you remember me? I've got some tasty food and medicine to give you. It's delicious. Much better than human meat."

Both dogs tilted their heads to the side and then they got up as if I hadn't spoken, passing right by me into the hallway. I held my breath as their tails whipped at my thighs and then followed them with my gaze until they got to the end of the hallway. They turned back and looked at me expectantly and I let out a whoosh of breath.

"Good doggies," I said, feeling a little more confident now that it seemed unlikely I was going to die. Sometimes things just worked out how they were supposed to. It wasn't a normal occurrence in my life, so I kept waiting for the other shoe to drop, but it was nice all the same.

CHAPTER NINE

WEDNESDAY...KIND of

The other shoe dropped about 5am when I woke from a deep sleep to the sound of growls and glass breaking.

"Oh, shit. Ohmigod. Don't kill him!"

I'd ended up bringing the dogs home with me. They'd looked so sad when I'd opened the door to leave, and Johnny Castle was holding his leash in his mouth, looking at me expectantly. I couldn't stand up under their scrutiny, so I'd gathered up all their supplies and put them in the back of the BMW. I wasn't going to mention to Nick what happened to the head rest in the backseat. Apparently Johnny Castle's medicine has some unfortunate side effects—like him wanting to eat everything in sight.

I hauled ass downstairs in one of Nick's T-shirts and my panties, and tripped on the bottom stair and went down hard, bashing my knee against the hardwood floor. It was pitch black except for the nightlight in the kitchen.

"Johnny Castle! Baby! No!"

I heard Nick's swears and the click-clack of claws

against the floors and then a yelp as they skidded to a stop. My knee throbbed and I reached up to turn on a light before carefully getting to my feet and putting weight on my leg.

"Ouch, ouch, ouch." I limped as quickly as I could toward the kitchen. Nick had come in through the garage door instead of the front.

"When did we get dogs?" Nick asked. His voice was calm, and I was pretty glad in that moment that he was trained not to panic. Because I could guarantee if our positions were reversed I'd be needing a diaper right about now.

"I meant to call you and warn you, but I fell asleep."

Actually, I'd gotten in the Whirpool and found a marathon of Designing Women on TV. Three hours later I was pruny, I felt almost human, and I'd decided I wanted to be Julia Sugarbaker when I grew up. And I'd forgotten all about calling Nick to warn him about the dogs once I'd slid beneath the sheets.

"These are Rosemarie's dogs. There wasn't anyone to take care of them after she got arrested."

"So you volunteered?"

"I kind of promised her. She caught me at a weak moment and she was kind of losing her mind because of the whole peeing in front of people thing."

"What's the big deal?"

"Only a man would say that. Believe me, going to the bathroom in front of others is a very big deal to women. We don't even like people in the stall next to us to hear what's going on. A girl learns early on how to covert pee."

"I don't even want to know what you're talking about. Can we get back to how we've ended up with two dogs that won't let me in my own home?"

I flipped on the overhead light in the kitchen and saw Nick was still pressed against the door. His weapon was out but relaxed at his side now that the dogs had stopped their attack. They sat about three feet in front of him, letting off the occasional growl and waiting for me to give them the command to attack.

It turns out Rosemarie's dogs love me.

"Are you hurt?" I asked.

"Not at the moment."

"Are you mad at me?"

"I'm taking it under consideration. Have you given the dogs our bed?"

"No, I gave them the room your grandfather stayed in when he visited at Thanksgiving. They like the bed. It's soft."

"Good. I won't change the sheets next time he comes to visit. He hates dogs. What'd you do to your knee?"

I looked down and saw it was swollen and already turning an interesting shade of purple. "Ya know. Testing out my ninja skills on the stairs."

"Looks like the stairs won. If you'll call the dogs off I'll get you an ice pack."

I pulled out one of the chairs from the kitchen table and sat down hard, propping my leg up on the opposite chair. "Baby. Johnny Castle. Go lay down in your room. Nick's one of the good guys."

They looked him up and down one more time and then looked back at me again just to make sure. I nodded my head in the affirmative and off they went, back to their room. They were really quite intelligent animals.

Nick let out a breath and rubbed his hands over his face. He looked awful, and I felt even guiltier for not remembering to warn him about the dogs. His clothes were rumpled, a coffee stain was on his shirt, he was way past a five o'clock shadow, and his eyes were bloodshot. He walked over to the freezer and pulled out a bag of frozen peas, and then leaned down to the fridge to grab a beer. He brought the peas over to set on my knee and then dropped down into the chair next to my propped up leg.

I hissed as the cold touched my skin, but it wasn't long before the throbbing started to dull a little. "You any closer to solving your case?" I asked.

"Got a tip just after ten o'clock and made an arrest around midnight. I've got to be up in a couple of hours and get back to the station to finish up. He'll be processed by then."

"Any news on Rosemarie?"

"I know her attorney showed up because Jacoby was bitching about it."

"I really hate Jacoby," I said, scowling.

"Most of us do too. He can be a real asshole. I didn't realize you knew each other."

"We don't. At least not in person. Do you think they'll release Rosemarie on bail in the morning?"

"More than likely. It's only a second degree charge and she has a clean record."

"Can you tell me anything new?"

"Honestly, I can't. I've been so swamped with my own case I haven't had time to catch up on the other. I'll check for you in the morning though."

"I've got to help her, Nick. She doesn't have anyone else."

"Or you could let the police do their job and stay out of trouble."

"No way. Jacoby wants her to be guilty. He even stole her emergency cache of M&Ms."

"I have no idea what that means. But that sounds like Jacoby." Nick stretched and then lifted the peas on my knee to take a closer look. "That's going to be stiff as hell in the morning."

"I guess it's a good thing I finished all my testing. I'm not sure Phoebe would've had enough drugs to get me through all that on a swollen knee."

"Your family terrifies me, sweetheart."

"The feeling is most definitely mutual."

CHAPTER TEN

I'M NOT sure what time Nick left the house, but it was still dark outside and I was still burrowed under the covers. I had every intention of taking my time after the grueling day before, and maybe taking another soak in the whirlpool, especially with my knee swollen to twice its usual size.

My cell rang just as I pulled Nick's shirt over my head and tossed it in the hamper.

"Yo," I said into the phone when I saw Savage's name appear in the caller ID.

"Yo, yourself. Get ready to roll. I'll swing by to pick you up in thirty. Wear something casual. And no high heels."

"I'm assuming this has to do with Khan?" I asked as I looked longingly at the tub. It wasn't going to happen this morning. I turned on the shower instead.

"Yeah, and our window of opportunity is very small. So be ready."

"I'm on it. And if you bring me a mocha latte in the biggest cup you can find I promise to be in a good mood."

"It's a deal. You were pretty scary yesterday."

He hung up without a goodbye and I tossed the phone on the counter. As long as I didn't put too much weight on my knee I was in good shape, so I gingerly made my way into the shower and washed as quickly as possible. There was no time to dry my hair, so I didn't wash it. It seemed like an excellent day to wear a hat.

The problem with the word casual is that it can mean a lot of things. Especially when a man is the one saying it. Does he mean wear sweats and tennis shoes or does he mean wear jeans and a nice blouse? There are varying degrees of casual.

I pulled jeans out of my closet first and found out very quickly that my knee was not going to fit through the leg hole.

"Yoga pants it is." I pulled a pair out of the drawer and then grabbed a loose sweater in baby blue. Tennis shoes were out of the question because I couldn't really bend over to tie the laces, so I opted for my black Uggs. I pulled my hair into a ponytail and slipped a black baseball cap on my head. I was downstairs and ready to roll with two minutes to spare. Savage was already in front of the house. Or at least I assumed it was Savage. He was in a white panel van with the words Speedy Cleaners painted on the side.

I grabbed my bag, made sure the dogs had water and food, and then hobbled out the front door as fast as my aching body would allow. Savage's brows raised as I opened the car door and ungracefully slid inside. I arched my own brow at the sight of him. He was wearing a pair of white coveralls and a baseball cap that said Speedy Cleaners just like on the side of the van.

"That limp could be a problem for our morning activities."

"I just need to walk on it a bit. It'll loosen up."

"If you say so. You were mostly in one piece when I left you yesterday. Do I want to know how this happened?"

"Probably not. Do you want to tell me why we're driving around in a Speedy Cleaners van and why you look like you're about to paint a house? I barely recognize you."

Savage pulled up his pant leg and I saw a pair of purple socks with palm trees all over them. "Recognize me now?" he asked.

"Yes, much better."

"I've got the boxers to match."

"I'll pass on seeing those."

"I figured we should pay Dexter Kyle a visit this morning. He's in court this morning, and Wednesdays are when his cleaning service shows up."

"Ahh. Let me guess. Speedy Cleaners?"

"The one and only. I manipulated their computers and put in an order to cancel the regular service. And with a little help from Byron I've got the security codes and a remote to disable the cameras."

"It pays to know people in the right places."

"That's pretty much the motto of anyone in law enforcement. And by the way, I don't have to remind you that what we're doing is technically illegal, so we want to stay under the radar."

"Got it. I can be very stealthy when I set my mind to it. Practically invisible."

"Yes, I remember how invisible you can be from the

last time we did a job like this together. Just don't break anything or draw attention to yourself."

I pinched my lips together and decided it was best not to argue. It's not like he wasn't right, but I thought it was pretty ungentlemanly to keep bringing it up. I was only human, after all.

"There's an extra set of coveralls behind you along with shoe protectors," Savage said. "Time to suit up."

I leaned around to look behind the seat and saw the neat stack of clothing, along with a Speedy Cleaner's hat and a pair of latex gloves.

"This should be interesting," I said, wondering how I was going to contort my leg enough to get it through the oversized leg holes. I bit my bottom lip and held back a whimper as I pulled it on, and I was glad Savage was smart enough not to make a comment. He was kind of a loose cannon at times, but his instincts were spot on.

I finally got the coveralls up and zipped and then bent down to put on the white booties that would protect the floors from my shoes. I exchanged my hat and then pulled on the gloves.

"I feel very...white," I said. "Speedy Cleaners could do with a little color in their life. Maybe a scarf or something."

"Yes, I'm sure all the cleaners would love a colorful scarf around their necks while they're scrubbing toilets."

"It never hurts to accessorize," I said primly.

Dexter Kyle lived just off Forsyth Park, not far from Nick's parents, in a narrow three-story house. It had a widow's walk and a red door, and the overgrown plants in the front garden were in serious need of maintenance. I wondered briefly if he let them grow wild for privacy. It was almost impossible to see the house or the windows from the street.

Savage backed into the driveway and I felt the little fireflies of adrenaline bouncing around in my stomach that appeared every time I was about to do something that might be slightly illegal. Mostly though, I was afraid of Kate. She had a hard rule at the agency that no one was to break the law. Not ever. Actually, I liked to think of it as more of a suggestion than a rule. And I also found it really important to keep all of these off the books B&E sessions to myself. I didn't want to lose my P.I. license before it had even come in the mail.

Savage got out of the van and pocketed the keys, sliding open the side door of the panel van and reaching inside for the vacuum and cleaning supplies. I let out a breath and then joined him on the driveway, taking a bucket and mop out of my side to carry in. My knee was throbbing like a bitch, and I was using the mop handle as a kind of cane to keep my balance. I wasn't doing a very good job of it.

"You're looking a little too much like Flavor Flav, babe. All you need is a big ass clock around your neck."

"Thank you. I've been working on my street cred."

Savage cracked out a laugh and positioned me once we got to the front door so I blocked his hands from view. It only took him a few seconds to pick both the lock and the deadbolt, and he swung the front door open and motioned me to enter.

The alarm beeped, signaling our thirty seconds before all hell broke loose, and Savage went to the control panel and punched in the code Byron had given him.

"What about the cameras?" I asked.

"Already taken care of." He pulled a remote no bigger than the palm of his hand out of his pocket.

"Fancy." I closed and locked the front door behind us just for good measure and then dropped my bucket on the floor and propped the mop against the wall.

"What happens if Dexter fires Speedy Cleaners because they didn't clean today?"

"Not our problem. Casualties of war."

"Remind me to never play games with you. You're too cutthroat."

"What kind of games are we talking about? Monopoly or the sexual kind? Because I can promise my reaction would be different depending on which you chose."

I clapped my hands together and ignored the way my pulse sped. "Alrighty then. I'm going to start on this floor, and you can take the upstairs. Let me know if you find anything."

"Just a minute, Mata Hari." Savage took hold of my arm, and I couldn't decide if he was serious or if he just wanted an excuse to touch me. "You hear that?"

Okay...so it wasn't an excuse to touch me. Good to know. I heard scratching against one of the doors and soft whimpers.

"It's just a dog," I said, letting out my breath in relief. I was feeling extra confident after my time with Baby and Johnny Castle. "Let me handle this. It turns out I'm just like the Dog Whisperer and didn't even know it."

"Be my guest."

I limped to a wood-paneled door just past the stairs. There was a formal living room with doors wide open just before it and an office that had lots of wood paneling and books on the opposite side. The house wasn't wide enough across to have too many rooms on each floor, and I was hoping we'd get lucky and find the Enterprise in the dining room.

From the sound of the scratches on the door the dogs weren't big. I couldn't tell how many there were, but I knew it was at least two.

"Hey, puppies," I said, using the same tone of voice I had with Rosemarie's dogs. The whimpers quieted on the other side of the door and I shot Savage a cocky grin. "I told you."

"I'd never have believed it if I hadn't seen it with my own eyes."

I narrowed my eyes and scrutinized his expression because I couldn't tell whether or not he was being sarcastic, but his face stayed suspiciously blank. I put my hand on the doorknob and turned it slowly, preparing to work my magic once more, but as soon as the door opened something small and furry flew right at me.

"Get it off! Get it off!" I yelled, spinning around as fast as my knee would allow.

The dogs were terriers of some sort, but looked more like overgrown rats. One of them had latched onto the extra fabric of my coverall that hung down below my crotch and the other was attached to my sleeve.

"Get these mutherfluffin dogs off of me!"

"You've gotta be still," Savage yelled back, but I could hear the laughter in his voice.

I shook my body back and forth, the dogs hanging on for dear life and swinging like mini rabid Tarzans, and Savage's laughter grew louder.

"You'd better not be laughing," I said. "Do something! Tase them for cripes sake."

"Are you sure you don't want to talk them down from the ledge, Dog Whisperer?"

My snarl at Savage was almost as loud as the dogs, and my knee chose that moment to give out. I went down in a heap at the bottom of the stairs, little paws wrapped around my arms and legs and sharp teeth tearing my clothes to shreds.

"This is not how I wanted to die," I wailed. "Death by cannibal dogs."

"You've got to hold still," Savage said again. "I can't get ahold of the little devils."

I tried to curl up in a little ball to protect myself better, but I don't know if I succeeded. My knee had a mind of its own.

"Tell my mother not to dress me in yellow for the funeral. She always made me wear yellow for school pictures when I was a kid because it was such a happy color. But it makes my skin sallow. And if I die I most assuredly won't be happy."

"I'll try to remember to tell her. Lord, you're loud."

I heard the rip of fabric and a snarl, and then the weight was suddenly gone from my body. I opened my eyes and saw Savage standing over me, his breathing slightly labored and a grin on his face. He had a dog tucked under each arm.

"I don't think Cesar Milan is going to be calling you up any time soon."

"If I wasn't such a lady I'd tell you to suck a bag of dicks right now. But I am, so I won't."

Savage barked out a laugh and shook his head at me. "Let me put them somewhere out of the way, and I'll help you up."

He turned away before I could mumble that I didn't need his stupid help. I could get up all by myself. In reality I probably looked like a turtle spinning around on its shell. Savage came back quickly and lifted me from under the arms, letting me use his body to steady myself once I was ready to put weight on my knee again.

"I've got good news and bad news," Savage said once I was back on my feet.

"What's the good news? I could use some."

"Spock's Enterprise is in a glass case in the dining room where the dogs were stashed."

"What's the bad news?"

"You're a terrible maid. Look at these floors."

I looked down and saw little shreds of cloth that had come from my clothes. There was also a broken picture frame and a small clock that had had the face popped off of it.

"Well, I was just keeping it real. I thought it was important for you to witness firsthand that I'm not perfect at everything."

"Mission accomplished, babe."

CHAPTER ELEVEN

AFTER THE DOG incident and finding the Enterprise exactly where it was supposed to be, the rest of our B&E was rather anticlimactic. Because we were breaking the law we couldn't exactly call in the big guns to come in and take it back, so we packed up our stuff and got back in the van.

When we got down to the corner Savage made a call on his phone and left an anonymous tip as to where the merchandise was located. I cringed to think what this meant for my part of the job and how I was supposed to be working for the insurance agency and not incriminating a federal judge who had the power to make my life a living hell if he ever found out I was behind it.

"You hungry?" Savage asked.

"Yes, but not hungry enough to eat wearing chewed up coveralls. And I'm pretty sure one of the dogs peed on me."

"I wasn't going to mention it because I thought it'd freak you out."

I sighed and tried not to gag. I found it weird that I'd

rather see blood or brain matter all day instead of normal bodily functions, but being peed on was pretty much where I drew the line. Even by a dog.

"I'm not going to freak out," I said. "Just take me to Phoebe's so I can grab a quick shower and borrow some clothes."

"Has anyone checked out your knee?"

"It'll be fine. I just need to stay off of it and keep it iced."

"Alternate between ice and heat. Have you talked to Kate?"

"Not exactly. I think it's best to avoid her, considering we just broke the law. You know how she gets. And technically she hasn't hired me as a fulltime agent yet, so I don't want to shake that apple cart."

Savage shook his head and grinned. "Listening to you guys talk is like learning a foreign language. What do apple carts have to do with Kate?"

"Hey, I've heard a y'all or two slip from your lips every now and then. You're not a Yankee anymore. Best to adapt."

"So, hypothetically speaking, if I took you to meet my family up north you'd stop saying bless your heart and making random references to your crazy Aunt Scarlet that always sits on the porch naked."

I arched a brow and pursed my lips. "Aunt Scarlet has taught me a lot of life lessons. I think she'd resonate across the Mason-Dixon Line. Also, I didn't realize you had parents."

Savage stared at me like I had two heads. "People have to come from somewhere. Of course I have parents. And a couple of brothers and a sister too."

"I know everyone comes from somewhere. I just

always assumed you hatched. Or maybe dropped to Earth from Krypton like Superman. I can't imagine you as a kid."

"Make that trip north with me and I'll show you all the baby pictures you want."

I hmmed non-committedly and looked out the window. Going anywhere with Savage was a bad idea.

We made it to Phoebe's house just in time to see her toss a couple of boxes into the back of her Jeep. Paintbrushes and canvas stuck out haphazardly and seemed to be mixed in with clothes and whatever else she could fit in.

"Well, fuck," I said. "Though I have to give her credit. She lasted longer than she usually does."

"So this is normal?"

"And expected. Phoebe has wanderlust. The minute she graduated high school she hit the road, and it's rare she comes back for any length of time like she did this time around. I was thinking maybe she was finally starting to grow up a little."

We parked the van next to her Jeep and I hobbled out.

"Good Lord, Addison," she said. "You look like something the cat dragged in."

"Close. Giant rats disguised as dogs."

"That would've been my second guess. Looks like they peed on you as a final insult. I can't believe you're not jumping around screaming. I know how you hate to be peed on." She turned and looked at Savage. "When she was seven we were visiting some cousins in Alabama and she walked right into a pissing contest between five boys. She about went catatonic. I've never seen anything like it. Those Alabama boys pee on everything, but I guess she didn't know that."

"I was seven, for Pete's sake. Not the worldly nine that you were."

"Worldly enough to not get pissed on."

"That's why we're here," Savage broke in before I could launch myself at Phoebe. PMS made me feel a little violent. "She needs a shower and a change of clothes."

"And maybe a bag of frozen peas if you have it," I added.

"I can fix you up. Though I don't think I have peas. Will corn work?"

"Only if it's frozen." Savage held out his arm, and for once I was grateful for the contact. He helped steady my weight and I limped along beside him, up the three stairs that led to the porch and then into the house I'd lived in for a short time. "So where are you headed?" I asked Phoebe.

"New York. I've got a show coming up. And I miss the city."

Phoebe was a painter. A pretty damn good one too. But it had surprised the hell out of all of us that she'd been able to make a success out of something she'd always considered a hobby.

"Are you keeping this place?"

"Well, technically the lease is in your name, so no. I've got an apartment set up in Soho that has a great loft with good light for my painting."

"Wonderful. What the hell am I supposed to do with this house when I'm living with Nick? There's another six months on the lease."

"Keep it. That way if you have a fight you won't have to move back home with mom and Vince. Goodness gravy, those two are loud. I don't ever remember her and daddy going at it like that."

"Can we please not talk about that while I'm covered in dog piss? I can only hold back the gag reflex for so long."

"This is the reason I moved several states away from my brothers and sister," Savage said.

"You have a family?" Phoebe asked.

I nodded and took the folded clothes she handed me. "That's what I said too. He said he was a child and everything."

"You guys are hilarious. Next time you need me to help you on a case maybe I'll reconsider."

"No you won't," Phoebe said. "You're putty in her hands."

"Are you really?" I asked, eyes wide. I was pretty sure I was flirting a little, but since I'd always been awful at flirting compared to Phoebe I couldn't be sure I was successful at it. I wondered how far was too far, because I could definitely use some help. With a bum knee, Rosemarie in the slammer, and not a whole lot of information to go on, I could use an ace up my sleeve to get to the bottom of Priscilla Loveshack's murder.

Savage sighed and gave me a wink. "Look at you with your snarled hair and pee-stained clothes. How could I resist?"

"Good," I nodded. "Hold that thought and I'll be right back. You too, Phoebes. I'm going to need your help."

"I'm not dressing up as a nun again," Phoebe said. "That turned out to be more trouble than it was worth. You'd think all those people would've noticed the beer in my hand while they asked me to pray for them."

I left Phoebe and Savage in the kitchen and made it to the bathroom on my own. Getting in and out of the shower could've been worse. I didn't fall and no one was videotaping my gracefulness as I hung onto the towel bars and prayed to God one didn't snap off and smack me in the face.

That had happened to the girl that lived in the apartment across from mine in college. She and her boyfriend were going at it like rabbits in the bathroom, her hands grasping the towel bar for all it was worth. Then all of a sudden it pulled free from the wall and whacked her right across the nose.

It had sure scared the hell out of me. I'd been studying in my room and then screams broke out and bloody naked people were running up and down the hall like it was an episode of The Walking Dead. Blood and sex don't really go together in the south. At least not in Georgia, but I've heard they've got one of those weird sex cults in Kentucky, so they might be more partial to the combination.

Anyway, that girl ended up with a broken nose and two black eyes, and no one ever heard from her boyfriend again. If you ask me, a man that runs away during any kind of sex is no man at all, but that's just my personal opinion.

I prayed a little extra for the towel rod to hold as I bear crawled over the edge of the tub because the last thing I wanted was a broken nose. I'd been blessed with a pretty good one and didn't feel like I needed to add any character to my face.

I somehow managed to soap myself off and wash my hair without killing myself. The trouble was going to be getting out of the shower.

I turned the water off and stifled a scream when Savage said, "Don't freak out," from the other side of the curtain.

"Jesus, Savage. Of course I'm going to freak out. Do you know how many times I watched Psycho as a kid?" My heart was racing a hundred miles a minute and I was clutching the shower curtain for all it was worth.

"I figured you might need some help getting out of the shower. Here's a towel if you want to wrap up first."

A towel appeared over the top of the curtain and I took it, drying myself carefully. Another towel came down and Savage said, "For your hair."

"Very thoughtful of you," I said, taking it and wrapping it like a turban around my head.

"I can be thoughtful at times."

I wasn't sure I liked seeing the sweeter side of Savage. As long as I could keep him in the reckless irresponsible box of my brain then I could tell myself he was only good as a friend.

I wrapped up with as much modesty as I could manage and then pulled the shower curtain aside. Savage had changed out of his Speedy Cleaners gear and was dressed in his normal jeans and black T-shirt. He wore Vibram-soled boots in case he needed to kick the crap out of anything and a black waterproof wristwatch that had more bells and whistles than I could keep track of.

"Dude. Your knee looks awful."

"You're such a flatterer," I said.

"Wow, I'm thoughtful and a flatterer. All of these compliments are going to start going to my head. Grab hold and I'll lift you out. No funny business though. I might drop you if you try to grab my butt."

I rolled my eyes and grabbed hold of his shoulders, trying not to notice how broad they were, or the muscles that bunched beneath my touch. And then he put an arm around my waist and another beneath my knees and lifted me up into his arms. My breath caught in my chest and the heat of desire tingled across my skin. I brought my hand up and thunked myself in the head.

"What was that for?" Savage asked.

"Just me being an idiot." Someday I would remember what happened to my body every time he put his hands on me and cut it off at the pass. Maybe. I might be an idiot, but I wasn't stupid.

He closed the toilet lid and set me down gently and then handed me the stack of clothes. "I'll be just outside the door, so call for help if you need it."

"Thanks, but I'd rather die a slow and painful death than have you come in while I'm half naked and tangled in my clothes."

"I'll just grab a beer then. Good luck."

Phoebe gave me yoga pants, a sports bra, and a grey hooded sweatshirt that seemed too plain for her wardrobe. But then I realized it was one I'd loaned her a couple of years before and all felt right with the world again. I pulled my snarled hair back in a ponytail and decided the bags under my eyes were mostly unnoticeable. And then I made my way back into the living room and fell back on the couch, exhausted.

"I'm going to need your help with Rosemarie," I said. "I can't leave her in that jail, and more importantly, I can't keep her dogs. They ate my backseat and almost ate Nick when he came home this morning."

"You do have a way with dogs," Savage said.

I arched a brow and chose to take the high road and ignore the comment. "Can you find out what's going on with the investigation?" I asked Savage. "Detective Jacoby is in charge, but I don't get the impression he's all that concerned with finding out the truth. Rosemarie's prints are on the murder weapon, and that's as good as an open and shut case as far as he's concerned. He's already charged and booked her."

"It's a good thing I'm on vacation," Savage replied. "I can find out what I can, but you know how tightlipped cops can be toward the Feds. It'd help if I could get a copy of his case files."

"Would they be on the computer?"

"Probably not. At least not this early in the investigation. It might be easier to start our own investigation and go from there."

"I like that option better. I'm full up on breaking and entering for the day. And I'd like to not do anything that might get Nick fired."

"Let's hit the road then. It sounds like they're moving fast with this one."

"Apparently the death of an ex-porn star reflects badly on the community."

"I saw her on that Discovery Channel special," Phoebe said. "She said she liked being a business woman much better than a porn star. Apparently when you have sex all day you have to go home and ice your privates to keep the swelling down. It sounds like selling dildos was much less stressful."

"Something to keep in mind if I ever decide to change careers." I took Savage's offered hand and got to my feet. "I'm ready. And as long as we can make a stop by Dairy Queen on the way. Then I'll be good as new. You want to come along?" I asked Phoebe.

"Are you going to the one on Memorial Drive?"

"That's the closest one."

"I'll pass then. Remember back when I was dating Roger Jeffries?"

"Vaguely. That was sixty-eight boyfriends ago, so it gets kind of blurry."

"It turns out he was dating Julie Rafferty at the same time, and I found out about it. By that time I didn't want him anymore, and I told Julie she could have him with my blessing. I think Roger was just relieved I didn't stab him with a sharpened paintbrush."

"The weapon of choice for artists everywhere," Savage added straight-faced, but I could see the humor lurking in his eyes. Phoebe was oblivious to subtle humor for the most part, so she just nodded and kept going with her story.

"Anyway, Roger and Julie went on about their relationship like I'd never even been in the picture, and then one day Roger up and had a stroke out of the blue, and now Julie is manager over at the Dairy Queen on Memorial."

"So what you're saying is that if people fuck you over then they might have a stroke," I said.

"All I'm saying is, karma can be a bitch. But I don't want to wave a red flag in front of the bull by showing up at the Dairy Queen with the two of you."

"Probably a wise decision. I'm not as nimble as I normally am and wouldn't be much help if you got in a fight."

"Because you'd be the person I'd call for backup if I was in a fight, even when you're in top form."

"Right. Good point. When are you leaving for New York?"

"Now. I'll leave the key under the mat. Can you tell mom for me?"

"No, I don't think so," I said, shaking my head. "Send

her an email. I don't want to have to listen to how she wishes you'd settle down for the next two hours."

I gave Phoebe a hug and wished her luck and then followed Savage outside. The wind had picked up and sleet was falling in earnest now, actually collecting on the ground instead of melting. That wasn't a good sign, because any time Savannah saw any accumulation of ice or snow—it didn't matter how small—the entire city shut down.

"Where's the van?" I asked, realizing the driveway was empty except for Phoebe's Jeep.

"I had someone come pick it up and remove the decals. We'll take my truck."

"Good. Don't forget the ice cream."

CHAPTER TWELVE

We drove back to the agency, me with a hot fudge sundae and Savage with a dip cone.

"I've got to stop hanging out with you. You're going to make me fat," Savage muttered.

"Nobody's forcing it down your throat."

"That's the thing about temptation. If you wave it around in front of a person long enough, eventually they give in to it."

His gaze was hot as it met mine and I felt the heat rush to my cheeks. I broke eye contact and looked down at my ice cream. Maybe enlisting the help of Savage wasn't the best idea, but I didn't have any other option until Rosemarie's name was cleared.

A parking spot magically appeared right in front of the agency and Savage parallel parked like a champ. He helped me hobble up the stairs, and I was starting to get a little impatient with the injury. I didn't have time for this. I shrugged off Savage's arm, determined to walk on my own.

"What's the plan?" I asked.

"Standard background check for starters. Let's see who her next of kin is and what her assets are. Checking out significant others and where the money leads is always the best place to start."

Lucy was away from her desk when we came in, but I saw my name written on a yellow sticky note attached to a file folder, so I grabbed it and tucked it under my arm.

"There you are," Kate said as we came around the corner. "Agent Savage," she acknowledged and then raised her brows at me.

I gave her a sheepish smile but didn't say anything. Sometimes keeping my mouth shut was the smartest thing I could do.

"I tried calling you yesterday, but you didn't pick up. Good job on the exams."

"Thanks. It was an eventful day, so I just went home and crashed."

She looked down at my knee. "Quite literally, it seems. I need to talk to you for a few minutes in my office."

I knew that tone. She wasn't upset, but she was curious about something and wanted to get to the bottom of it. I wondered briefly if I had a chance of escaping if I made a run for it, but my stupid knee was going to hold me back. I was easy pickings.

"I'll meet you down there. I need a minute with Savage."

"I'll find you if you try to run," she said.

I smiled and batted my eyelashes. "Why would I try to run? I haven't done anything wrong." Except for tampering with a case and a little illegal breaking and entering, but how could she possibly know about that?

"Uh huh," she said and went back to her office.

I turned to Savage. "My office is just through there. Feel free to use whatever you need while I talk to Kate."

"10-4, kemosabe."

I hoofed it as fast as I could down to the far end of the hall where Kate's office was located, but Jimmy Royal stuck his head out his office door and shouted, "Hey, Holmes. Looks like your streak is over. And you were doing so well, too."

"Up yours, Jimmy. I can't believe you don't have something better to do than count down the days until I get injured."

Jimmy was an ex-cop and second in command at the agency. He was just over six feet tall and thin as a beanpole. He always wore cowboy boots and his eyes reminded me of a basset hound.

Since I'd started working for Kate he'd taken to hanging a chalkboard outside of his door proclaiming to the world how many days I'd gone without injuring myself. Today the number was at 22. He was right. I'd had a pretty good streak going. I'm not sure I'd ever made it that long before. Which depressed the hell out of me the more I thought about it. Maybe I should buy stock in Tylenol.

Jimmy chuckled. "Darlin,' you know I live for these days. What'd you do this time? Fall off a roof? A bar brawl? Did you wrestle a grizzly?"

I shot Jimmy the finger and kept moving toward Kate's office. Cops had a weird sense of humor. I knocked on Kate's door once out of habit but let myself inside. She was lounging in one of the club chairs in the sitting area instead of behind her desk and I went over to join her. It wasn't often I saw Kate relaxed.

"When was the last time we went out and did

something fun? Just the two of us, like we used to. Something that has nothing to do with work."

"Two weeks ago we went to that movie theater that had the waiters and food service. We drank almost two bottles of wine, ate spaghetti, and had a lot of popcorn. You cried through the whole movie. Loudly."

"Oh yeah. That night is kind of a blur. Sometimes the animated movies are the most emotional. And don't play tough with me, Kate McClean. I saw you dabbing your eyes with the hem of your shirt."

"Hmm," she said, picking an invisible piece of lint off her slacks. "It's the old people. Any time a movie has old people and they get all nostalgic it makes me weepy. We're going to be there one day, you know."

"Not me. I'm going to be an awesome old lady. Balls to the wall. I'm going to wear ridiculous hats and say just what I want, no matter how controversial. And maybe I'll get a motorcycle and get a lover twenty years younger than me."

"So you're going to turn into your mother?"

I opened my mouth to refute it, but then snapped it closed again. "My mother isn't old yet. She's still in her early fifties and has years to mellow into a respectable geriatric. What did you want to see me about?"

"I meant what I said in the hallway. Congratulations on doing so well on the exam. I honestly didn't think you'd be able to pull it off. Especially the physical fitness portion. I know you struggled with that."

I pressed my lips together and smiled, deciding it probably wasn't a good idea to mention that Phoebe had medicated me.

"So I guess I'm officially offering you a job as a fulltime agent, if you still want it. Once your license comes in you can officially hang it in your office and be open for business."

"Can I have a bigger office?"

"No. But if anyone dies or retires you'll be the first to get an upgrade."

"I can live with that. I've got to get back to Savage. I suppose you heard about Rosemarie."

"Yeah, it's a shame. I can't imagine she's handling it well. But I heard she's getting bonded out this morning. She might already be out."

I started to push off the couch and make my escape, but Kate said, "So what's going on between you and Savage? If I'd been standing any closer to you two out there I would have felt the sparks."

"Nothing is going on. I'd never cheat on Nick. And we are in a committed, adult relationship."

"And Savage is setting your panties on fire every chance he gets."

I deflated and fell back onto the couch. "Oh, yeah. That man is not good for me. But Lord, the temptation. I hope God gives me a medal for abstaining when I get to heaven one day. Because holy cow, I want to do all kinds of sinning with that man."

"Yes, I'm sure He will. Mother Theresa, Gandhi, Martin Luther King Jr.—and then you at the end of the line accepting your medal for not having sex with a testosterone-driven hot guy. I can see the parallels."

"Well, when you put it that way—"

Kate laughed and I grinned at her.

"So is there anything you want to tell me about why Standard Insurance would call me this morning and tell me to drop the case on Leonard Winkle?"

"Oh, really?" I asked innocently. That was just like

Kate. Soften you up and then come in for the kill. She was sneaky like that. "Good for Leonard. He didn't seem like the kind of guy who'd try to cheat an insurance company."

"Uh, huh. It turns out someone called in an anonymous tip about Judge Dexter Kyle being in possession of the stolen property. He's got so many people in this town in his pocket, including a few cops and the mayor, that it took a while for anyone with enough balls to get over there and check things out. I heard through the grapevine that Kyle is out for blood. He's not a man to mess with. He'll burn the whole city just to take down the one person who fucked him over."

I heard the warning in Kate's voice and acknowledged it. "Good to know." I smiled brightly and got to my feet. "I'm wasting daylight. I'd better get back to Savage." Kate raised her brows and I corrected myself. "I mean back to work."

"Right. I knew that's what you meant."

My phone rang as I walked back toward my office and I had to dig around in my bag to find it. I hit the connect button and had the phone to my ear to say hello when I noticed Jimmy Royal had changed the 22 on his sign back down to 0. I scowled and then realized someone was trying to talk to me.

"Addison, are you there?"

"I'm here. How are you doing, sweetie? The dogs are all taken care of and comfortable, so no worries there."

I heard Rosemarie's sigh of relief. "I was worried. They don't always take kind to others and sometimes they eat things when they're nervous. Johnny Castle once ate all the underwear in my drawer plus the wooden knobs. I shudder to even remember it. I was picking up lacy poop for days."

I scrunched my nose in disgust and saw Savage come out of my office, a stack of printed paper in his hand. He raised his brows at me in question and I mouthed Rosemarie's name. He nodded and leaned against the wall to wait for me to finish.

"Did you get bonded out?" I asked.

"Yeah, that's why I'm calling. I'm standing on the front steps of the courthouse. Could I catch a ride? My car is still in impound. They're looking for bloodstains or something."

"No problem. Savage and I are at the agency. Just meet us out front."

The courthouse was just across the way from the agency, so all in all it was a pretty convenient location. Unless it was peak rush hour and you needed to get anywhere in a hurry.

I disconnected the phone and headed toward Savage. "That was Rosemarie. They just bonded her out and she needs a ride. I told her it wouldn't be a problem. Did you find anything of interest?"

"A few things," he said. "Priscilla Loveshack's real name is Winnie Mayhew."

"Good gravy. No wonder she changed it."

"She's also a Savannah native. She's lived here her whole life."

I gasped and put my hands on my hips in disgust. "Are you telling me the Discovery Channel lied about her being from LA?"

"If you can't trust the TV, then who's left to trust?" Savage said straight-faced.

"Wait a minute. She made all her movies somewhere.

She can't have lived here her whole life. She's got more than two hundred and twenty film credits to her name. Including Bringing up Bambi 1, 2, and 3. Those looked like they might even have a plot to them."

"Should we watch for research?"

"Do you need a knuckle sandwich today?"

"I'll pass. And to answer your question, she made every one of those movies right here in Savannah."

"Shut the front door! Savannah has a porn industry?"

"A booming one, apparently. They pay taxes and have all their permits."

"I just can't believe it." I was in complete shock. To think I could've been sitting in my office at the agency and then right next door there could be a whole covert world of porn stars and fluffers. It was unthinkable. "So what are we going to do?"

"Priscilla was married and has two children in college who are still living at home. Why don't we start there and talk to whoever we can."

"Sounds like a plan."

We headed outside and Rosemarie was waiting next to Savage's truck. I had to do a double take to make sure it was her. I'd never seen her without makeup before.

In less than twenty-four hours she'd managed to embrace the look of prison—sallow skin and bags under her eyes. Her hair lacked sheen and was pulled back into a ponytail at the nape of her neck, and her eyes tracked everyone on the street nervously, like she was waiting for someone to jump out at her. She wore a lime-green fleece jogging suit that seemed much too bright next to her prison skin, and a quilted puffy coat that didn't quite meet in the middle so she could zip it up.

"I feel like everybody's staring at me," she whispered

as we got closer. "Now I know just how that Hester Prynne felt with her Scarlet Letter. Only I need a big fat M—an M for murderer."

I was thinking twenty-four hours in jail had sent Rosemarie right over the edge. That woman needed a massage and a manicure like no one I'd ever seen before. That would get her back on track.

"Let's dial back on the whole murderer thing," I said. "And maybe get you a cup of coffee. Savage and I are on the case. We'll have your name cleared in no time."

"I don't know. Detective Jacoby seems pretty certain. He almost had me convinced that I did it. If Maxwell hadn't been there I probably would've signed a confession."

"Jacoby?" Savage asked. "I hear he's a real asshole."

"I wouldn't mind slashing his tires if the circumstance presented itself," I chimed in.

"It's still early in the day. Come on. Let's get Rosemarie some coffee and take her back home."

We all piled into Savage's truck, and it was fortunate it had a roomy backseat. It was also fortunate it had good ventilation, because Rosemarie smelled like she'd been doused in disinfectant and my eyes started to water as soon as we closed all the doors.

I could tell Savage noticed it too because his eyes got real big and he started blinking rapidly. He eventually ended up cracking all the windows about an inch and we huddled deeper into our coats and ignored the tiny plops of ice that occasionally hit us in the face.

"Is that my mother?" I asked as we drove down Broughton Street. Her hands were full of shopping bags and she was looking up and down the road as if she were waiting for someone.

I thought I heard Savage groan, but he pulled the truck over to the side of the road and I rolled the window down all the way.

"Mom? What are you doing?"

"Oh, Addison. You scared me to death. I'm always worried that when a car comes up beside me someone is going to jump out and snatch me right off the street." She leaned in the window and looked around me at Savage. "Nice to see you again, Matthew."

"Mrs. Holmes," Savage said, nodding. "Do you need some help?"

"Not really. I went shopping with Betsy Guerke this morning and we were going to go to lunch afterward, but we got in an argument over that show Naked and Afraid. Have you ever seen that? It's the most ridiculous thing. Two naked people wandering around the woods and letting the ticks latch on to their privates like it was their very own genital buffet. I told Betsy the whole thing had to be staged, because who in their right mind would do that on purpose, but she got all hot and bothered and insisted it was real. Then she drove off without me. I was going to try to catch a cab."

I looked over at Savage and saw he was biting down hard on the inside of his cheek, but he managed to keep a straight face. Savage and Nick were both much better at concealing their emotions than I was.

"Get in, mom. We'll drop you off. We've got to take Rosemarie home anyway."

"Thank you. I accept."

Rosemarie scooted to the other side of the seat, and my mom got in, shuffling packages until they were so crammed in the backseat I wondered if Savage could even see out the rearview mirror.

"Good Lord. It smells like a morgue in here," my mother said. "What is that smell?"

"It's possible it could be me," Rosemarie said. "I just got out of prison."

"Did you get a tattoo? I heard they make you get those teardrops under your eyes when you murder someone."

"I haven't gotten one, but I was thinking about it. It's important to show how tough you are when going in. Otherwise you end up as somebody's bitch."

Savage went through the drive-thru line at the Starbucks and gave everyone's order. I'd decided on coffee —black—because I needed all the help I could get at this point.

"Savage and Addison are going to help prove my innocence," Rosemarie told my mother as she sucked down her caramel macchiato.

"Then you'll be right as rain in no time. Did I ever tell you I went on a job with Addison once? We had trench coats and everything, just like real spies."

Savage looked over at me and arched a brow, and I casually scratched my eye using my middle finger. That finger had gotten a workout lately.

"What kind of leads do you have?" my mother asked.

"We're going to start by interviewing family. It turns out Priscilla Loveshack is a Savannah native and has lived here all her life. She's got a house over in Chatham."

My mother and Rosemarie both gasped in unison. "That can't be true," my mother said. "It said plain as day on that Discovery Channel special that she was from LA. That's where she made all her movies."

"It turns out they were lying," I said, shrugging.

"Well, I'll be. You can't trust anyone these days."

"It also turns out that she made all her movies right here in Savannah."

"Isn't it something to think you could be shopping for a Sunday barbecue at the Piggly Wiggly and right next door someone could be making *Bringing up Bambi 4*?" I could almost feel my mother shaking her head in wonder. "I almost rented the first three, you know. Seems like they had a good plot, and I wanted to see what happened next. They really hook you in with those teasers."

I couldn't say I didn't understand where she was coming from, but that didn't mean I wanted to think about my mother watching porn. Hearing it coming from her room in surround sound was bad enough.

"Are you going to check out those places to see if you can find the real murderer?"

"If we can find them," I said. "That's why we're going to speak to her family first."

"It's a good thing Betsy left me high and dry. I don't have any plans for the rest of the afternoon, so I'm free to go with you."

"Oh, me too!" Rosemarie said, bouncing a little in her seat.

Savage was already shaking his head no and I felt all the blood rush from my head and straight to my feet.

"The thought of going home and facing my neighbors depresses the hell out of me. And you know that nasty old Iris Clarke is going to bring a coffee cake and pretend she gives a shit, just so she can find out information firsthand to spread around."

I'd been this close to denying them, but I caught myself after Rosemarie's explanation. It would be awful for her. And the neighbors would be so sugary-sweet with malice that you could sprinkle them on a bowl of cereal.

I looked at Savage with apology and then said, "Sure, you can come. But you have to stay in the car. Priscilla's family won't want to talk to us if they think you murdered her."

"I'm okay with that. I really just want to go to the movie set. I've never met an actor before."

"I'm not really sure they qualify as actors," I said.

"You think they have a gift shop?" my mother asked. "We could all get souvenirs."

"Or Savage could spare us all and drive off the Talmadge Memorial Bridge," I murmured.

"Sounds like a plan to me," Savage said just as quietly.

CHAPTER THIRTEEN

Priscilla Loveshack lived in a swanky neighborhood not far from the Savannah National Wildlife Refuge. The neighborhood was heavily treed and an old man sat inside a heated guard house and let people in and out if they were supposed to be there. Fortunately, Savage had a badge, even if he was supposed to be on vacation.

"I could live here," Rosemarie said. "I'm thinking I should probably move out of Whiskey Bayou. I can only imagine what kind of pariah I'm going to be. You remember when Jenni Skaggs got caught shoplifting all those plastic flowers at the home goods store? They blackballed her at every business in town. She had to come all the way to Savannah just to get gas and groceries. The whole business made her so angry she ended up burning down her house and moving across the country."

"That's not how it happened," my mom said, shaking her head. "She burned down her house cause she forgot to take her antidepressants. But she was on the antidepressants because of being blackballed, so I guess it's one and the same. It's all a downward spiral."

Priscilla's house was at the end of a cul-de-sac and sat like a big white elephant among the other homes in the neighborhood. It looked like a miniature replica of the White House, and I was dying to know what kind of decorating taste a porn star would have.

That question was answered as soon as Savage pulled into the long stretch of driveway and got closer to the house. All of the shrubs were pruned into different poses from the Kama Sutra.

"I didn't know box hedges could do such a thing," Rosemarie gasped, her hand coming to her mouth.

"I feel a little like Alice in Wonderland," my mother said. "If Alice fell down the rabbit hole and ended up in a sex garden."

"I'll leave the truck running," Savage said before the conversation could spiral downhill again. "Please don't get out, and definitely don't speak to anyone. Technically we're not even supposed to be here."

My mother nodded in agreement and Rosemarie saluted. I just sighed and shook my head, because there was about as much chance of them listening as winning the lottery.

I made sure I was careful on the driveway, because the sleet had made everything a little slick. If this kept up the whole city would be shut down before nightfall. As it was, there wasn't a hint of sun in the sky and the gray clouds looked angrier and more turbulent with every passing minute. It was a little disconcerting to walk past the phallus-shaped hedges as they iced over. There was something very unnatural about it all.

Just as we approached the columned porch and

massive front doors a team of gardeners rushed from the side yard with white trash bags and began to cover all of the sculptures. A small man followed behind them dressed in khakis, work boots, and a denim jacket, yelling in a constant stream of Spanish. Then he saw us.

"Hey, you!" he said, and I would've jumped if Savage hadn't put his hand on my elbow. "Get out of here. This is private property. I call the police. We don't need your kind around here being nosy."

"Our kind?" I asked Savage, confused. "What kind are we?"

"The nosy kind." Savage held up his badge and the little man stopped a few paces away. With the momentum he'd been using I'd been afraid he was going to steamroll right over us. "FBI. What's your name?"

"Hector Ortiz. I'm the head gardener here at Palacio del Blanco."

"Good name," I said. "Very fitting." Savage squeezed a little harder on my elbow and I zipped my lips.

"You're here about Mrs. Mayhew's murder?"

It took me a second to remember that Priscilla Loveshack was in all actuality Winnie Mayhew.

"That's right. Is Mr. Mayhew at home?"

"Oh, yes. And both of the children. They're planning the funeral. It is a very stressful time for the family. The police were already here."

"I'm investigating a different avenue. How long have you worked here?"

"Seven years. Mrs. Mayhew was very particular about her garden sculptures, and I knew just how she liked them."

If Savage's grip got any tighter I was going to have bruises. I was ninety percent good at knowing when to keep my mouth shut. I guess it was the other ten percent Savage was worried about.

"So you were working for her before she retired from the industry?"

Hector hesitated for a moment, and I liked him for that. He'd been a loyal employee despite her chosen profession.

"Sí. She only took her retirement two years past."

I looked around the expansive gardens and house once more. "She had a very successful career."

"Oh, yes. Mrs. Mayhew was an excellent businesswoman. Her investments were quite good."

"Did they always film in the same location?" Savage asked.

Hector shrugged. "I don't think so. They moved around depending on what setting they were looking for. They even filmed here a couple of times, though she'd have gotten in trouble with the neighborhood if anyone had found out. But Mr. Elias was insistent, and at that time she still worked for him."

"Mr. Elias?"

"Travis Elias. He's the owner of Purgatory Studios and the money man."

"Thanks for your time, Mr. Ortiz. You've been very helpful. And I'm sorry for your loss."

"Thank you," he said, nodding. "You're the first one who's said so. The other cop acted like she didn't matter because of who she was. But she was a fine lady."

We made it the rest of the way to the front door, and Savage hit the doorbell.

"Is that really playing Stairway to Heaven?" I asked.

"The rich get all the cool stuff."

I had to stifle a snicker when the door opened

suddenly. My eyes widened at the man who posed himself artfully against the door. He wore white cashmere pants and a matching sweater, and his white-blond hair hung past his shoulders. His skin was tanned and his eyes a pale blue. I was pretty sure I'd seen this man on several of the romance novels my mother kept in her bookshelf.

"Can I help you?" he asked. "This is a very inconvenient time for visitors."

His accent was Nordic. Or maybe Romanian. Or possibly a cross between the two, which led me to believe it was fake.

"I'm Agent Savage with the FBI, and this is Addison Holmes. We'd like to ask you a few questions regarding your wife."

He stared at us for a few seconds and then broke into a blindingly white grin. He clapped his hands together. "You are very good. You almost had me." He chuckled again and slapped his leg. "I'm not taking auditions at this time, but you should come back." He looked Savage up and down. "Nice build and a face that won't make the ladies run away screaming. That's the case, half the time. Once I see your goods and you do a screen test we can see what we can do about securing a role for you."

It wasn't often I got to see Savage speechless, but I was pretty sure this was one of those times. And then he turned to me and did the same up and down treatment. "You can do your screen test with your lady friend here, if it's convenient. She's not bad either. And she's a brunette. We're always running low on brunettes. What's your cup size, sugar? My trained eye tells me you're a C, but winter clothes can be so bulky. Are you waxed? Bald is in, you know. Best take care of that if you haven't already."

"Mr. Mayhew," Savage said again. "I really am with

the FBI. We'd really like to get to the bottom of your wife's murder."

"Are you serious? You're not here to be film stars?"

"No."

"Well that's a crying shame. I thought maybe I'd just discovered this decade's new star. My name is Lance, by the way." He left the door open and left us to follow, his hair floating behind him like a cloud.

"Of course his name is Lance," I whispered.

"A C cup, huh?" Savage asked. "My favorite."

"Shut up." I hunched my shoulders and followed the hair cloud.

Everything from the floors, to the furniture, to the doorknobs was white. It was blinding. But more startling than the lack of color were the giant portraits that graced the walls.

"And next to the definition of narcissism in the dictionary is a picture of this house," I said. "Wow. They really like to look at themselves."

Lance's portraits were of him in various stages of undress, as well as in costumes from different time periods, but his hair was always the same. There were several frames covered with a black cloth, and I had to assume these were the pictures of the late Mrs. Mayhew.

"We'll do this in the parlor," Lance called back. "It's the most relaxing room. I feel very Zen there."

"Jesus," I whispered as soon as we walked into the parlor.

A wall mural decorated one entire side of the room, and it was another painting of Lance, though this time his lance was fully erect and about to sheath itself in Priscilla Loveshack's scabbard. I had no idea why he was wearing a pirate hat and holding an Indiana Jones-style bullwhip during coitus, but I'd learned in life that sometimes there were no explanations. I also wondered if the picture was painted true to size, because holy moly that thing was not natural. My vagina cringed in sympathy, and it took every power I had not to let my gaze stray down the real Mr. Mayhew.

"Can I interest either of you in a brandy? It really heats the belly on days like today." He went over to a cart near the mural wall and posed again as he was pouring his drink.

"Oh, for cripes sake," I hissed.

"Did you work with your wife in films?" Savage asked.

"Oh, sure. That's how we met. On the set of Schindler's Naughty List. We were together almost twenty years."

I wasn't even going to get into the logistics of how that worked, considering Priscilla had made over two hundred adult films and most of them weren't with her husband. But I guess if it worked for them...

"I had my modeling career before that," he continued, "but I retired from that life because the films were more lucrative. At least until my injury." He looked away abruptly and took a long swallow of brandy as if he were following cues on set. I was thinking Mr. Mayhew probably hadn't been given very many speaking lines in his adult films.

Don't ask about the injury, Addison. No matter how curious you are. And then I realized I probably wouldn't have to ask. There was no way he was letting that go without an explanation.

"I fell off a fire truck during the filming of BackShaft and fractured my vertebrae in my lower spine. That's where all the thrusting power comes from, and by the time I recovered I was already a has-been."

"Who would've known," I said, laying on my accent a little thicker than normal.

"Where were you when your wife was killed, Mr. Mayhew?"

"I was here, of course. The children are home from college for the holidays, and we were all here together. Tucked snug into bed at that time of night."

"You didn't oppose your wife working at that time of night?"

"She didn't usually work the store, but both her manager and the salesgirl both called in sick with the flu and she didn't have anyone else to cover. Prissy was never one to let a dollar go to waste, so instead of closing, she opened the store herself. Sunday nights are big business. The after church sinners."

"Did she contact you that night? Did she seem worried?"

"We talked just before I took my Ambien at nine o'clock. That was the last time I ever heard that sexy voice."

Lance burst into tears and I rolled my eyes. I hadn't realized how drama free my family life was until I'd met Lance Mayhew.

"Where can we find Travis Elias?" Savage asked. Nothing much fazed Savage. Which was good, because it was important that one of us looked like a professional.

"Travis? Oh, he's here and there. They're filming on one of the riverboats this week."

"Which boat?"

"I don't know the name of it, but you'll recognize it when you see it. They tie black silk scarves along the gangplank to let the crew know where to go, and a guy the size of a monster truck guards the entrance."

"You've been very helpful, Mr. Mayhew." Savage took my elbow and guided me back toward the door. "Are you and your children the sole inheritors of your wife's estate?"

"As far as I know, but the will won't be read until Saturday. Would you like my autograph before you leave?"

CHAPTER FOURTEEN

When we got back to the truck, both of the back doors were open and mom and Rosemarie were still in their seats.

"What's with the doors?" I asked.

"That disinfectant smell was making me nauseous," my mother answered. She waved an old church bulletin that must have been inside her purse in front of her face. "I can't even imagine what that stuff does to the skin."

"What did you find out?" Rosemarie asked. "Is he guilty?"

"It's a little too soon to tell," I said. "But we have a film location. Apparently they're filming on one of the riverboats."

"Maybe they're doing a Showboat parody."

"Isn't that something?" my mother said. "Do you think they'll sing Ol' Man River?"

"I certainly hope not," I said. "I can't imagine anyone being able to find their rhythm with that song playing in the background. Maybe if they sped it up a little and added more bass."

"It's important to have a good rhythm in bed," Rosemarie said. "I dated a man once who couldn't find the beat if you hit him upside the head with it. Made me seasick, stopping and starting like that. It was like his penis had a stutter. Couldn't decide whether it was coming or going."

Savage turned onto East Bay Street and we made our way toward the docks. Parking was always a bitch down in this area, and my knee was screaming at the thought of traversing the uneven ground. But no sooner had I had the thought than a parking space as close as we could possibly get opened up right in front of us.

"Good grief," I said. "Does that always happen?"

"Pretty much."

We made our way to where several riverboats were docked. It wasn't difficult to figure out which one belonged to the porn stars. Pirate flags flapped in the whipping wind and someone had lined cannons along the top deck near the railing.

"It looks like they're filming a period piece," my mother said.

Rosemarie clucked her tongue. "I've always enjoyed pirates. I love those books where the dastardly pirate kidnaps the girl and they set sail across the high seas. Only while I'm reading I pretend they have fresh water and take a bath every day."

Mom nodded her head up and down like Rosemarie was preaching the gospel. "Good hygiene is essential for my fantasies too. Unless it's one where you've both been to the gym and had a good workout, getting those endorphins going and sweating like pigs. And then at the end he throws you down on the mat and has his way with you."

Mom and Rosemarie both started fanning their faces. Savage was staring straight down at his shoes with his hands on his hips, and I was wondering how much I'd have to work out if I added whiskey to my hot fudge sundae.

We started toward the gangplank and the large man that stood guard crossed his arms over his gigantic chest and spread his tree trunk legs wide. He was pale as a cue ball and had white-blond hair that fuzzed across his scalp like a Chia Pet. He wore a patch over one eye and the other was so dilated that I could barely see the ring of blue on the outside. I was thinking Pirate Pete was on some heavy pharmaceuticals.

"My goodness," Rosemarie said. "Aren't you a big one."

He looked down at Rosemarie and gave her a goofy grin. Maybe he wasn't so tough after all.

"Lance Mayhew told us to come on over," Savage said to the guard. "Sorry we're late."

By the grace of God my mother and Rosemarie stayed silent and let Savage continue with his lies. My mom was pretty much the worst liar in existence, but to her credit she knew this about herself, so she took the opportunity to start digging in her purse for a piece of gum.

"You're the new actors?" He looked us over from head to toe and apparently the sight of us didn't compute in his drugged out brain, because he had to do it a second time. His gaze stopped on my mother and I said a quick prayer that he didn't ask her a direct question.

"You one of the bunnies?" he asked her.

"This is my mother," I said before mom could stutter her way through a lie. "She's very supportive of my career. She comes to work with me all the time."

"Dude, that's weird. I guess go on up. Your mom will have to stay in the green room though. Only actors and production crew on set. But there's a TV in there if she really wants to watch."

Pirate Pete moved out of our way and we trooped up the gangplank and onto the ship.

"Addison, you know I've always been very open and honest with you girls about sex. I didn't want you growing up uncomfortable with your bodies or think that anything shared between a man and a woman in the bedroom was somehow wrong, because that's how I was raised. Lord, your grandmother couldn't even say the word sex without whispering it and turning five shades of red. But as comfortable as I've tried to make the subject over the years, I've got to tell you, the idea of going to work with my daughter to watch her shoot porn is a little weird. I think that's where I have to draw the line."

"It's good that you know what your limits are," I said. "I wasn't sure you had any."

We followed Savage up two sets of narrow steps. There were signs taped to the walls with arrows pointing in the direction of the different taping areas. I was actually rather surprised at the quality. I was expecting lots of red velvet and body fluids dripping from every available surface. It mostly just looked like a cruise ship, minus the free soft serve machines.

One of the wood-paneled side doors opened and a woman came out dressed in a thin silk robe. It was obvious she wasn't wearing anything underneath it, and I had to give Savage credit for keeping his eyes on her face and not wandering south.

I didn't have the same compunction. I looked her over from head to toe and then some. Her breasts defied gravity and she was so thin I could see her ribs through the robe. Bleached bottle hair couldn't hide the dark roots, and mascara was smudged under her cornflower blue eyes. I wanted to give her a moist towelette and offer her a cheeseburger.

Savage sent her a devastating grin, but she didn't seem all that impressed. After seeing that Discovery Channel special I could understand it. One of the porn stars said it got to the point that if she even saw a man heading in her direction she'd start running the other way. Apparently sex could get old. Which seemed like a bummer, because it was one of my favorite pastimes.

"Can you tell me where Travis Elias is? I need to check in with him."

She shrugged and looked at Savage with bored eyes. "He's catching up on business in the office on the top deck. You filming today, sugar?"

"So it seems. Got the call this morning from Lance Mayhew. I can't believe he can keep focused on the business after what happened to his wife."

She shrugged again and her robe slipped off one shoulder. "That's Lance for you. Nothing gets in the way of business. Especially not his wife's death. They hated each other anyway, so it's not like it's a big loss to him. I'm Pepper, by the way. Are you shooting the Walk the Plank scene? Cause that one is mine. I can show you around if you'd like."

"That'd be great, after I see Travis."

Pepper was showing a little more interest in Savage now, and I felt my hackles rise. I had no idea why. It's not like Savage was going to run off with an anorexic porn star. And even if he did, it wouldn't be any of my business, because Savage and I weren't in a relationship. And we weren't going to be in a relationship.

"I heard Lance is going to inherit a fat stack of cash. Must be nice."

Pepper laughed and reached into her robe pocket, pulling out a bottle of water and unscrewing the top. "Isn't that just the luck? Those who don't deserve it are the ones who end up with the windfall. I had to work with Lance a couple of times, and let me tell you, there's not an actress talented enough in the world to make it look like he's getting you off. I spent most of my time making mental grocery lists and deciding whether or not I wanted to take some classes at the community college.

"Priscilla was the real brains of that operation." She took a long drink of water and never let her gaze leave Savage's. "She's what all of us aim to be. But doing it how she did made her plenty of enemies. Let's just say none of us were real surprised to hear she was dead."

"It's a rough business," Savage said, just as casually.

I sure learned one thing during the conversation. Savage was an excellent liar. To the point that it kind of made me a little distrustful of him. How many times had he lied to me before and I'd never picked up on it?

"It takes balls to blackmail your way to freedom." Pepper finally looked at me and raised a penciled brow.

I was focusing on keeping my face free of surprise about the blackmail thing. It was starting to look like that cable special on porn stars had all been a big crock of shit.

"Are you the new girl?" she asked.

I knew I wasn't near hard enough to carry off the look of a seasoned porn star. I didn't have enough cynicism. And my breasts weren't quite at the right height. And my knees popped whenever I walked up the stairs, and it probably wasn't the best idea for me to spend a lot of hours on them.

"Yep," I said. "Excited to get started."

"That'll fade fast enough. The money isn't that good."

"I brought my mom and a friend for support. Maybe you could show them to the green room while we meet with Travis?"

"I've heard of a lot of fucked up things happening on these sets, but never have I seen anyone bring their mother along for a taping. That ain't right, girl."

My smile was more of a grimace and I nudged my mom when I saw her nodding in agreement out of the corner of my eye. Pepper led them both away and I shot Savage a look.

"Not bad, Holmes. You even managed to keep your face from broadcasting everything you were thinking. It looks like all those P.I. classes have been paying off."

I hmmmed and followed him up another set of narrow stairs to get to the top level of the riverboat. The wind was considerably stronger this high up, and rain and sleet blew down the long narrow hallway and dampened our faces and clothes.

I could see Travis Elias working inside a glass-enclosed room that had an old-timey looking helm and then more modern technology behind it that actually powered the riverboat when they took it out on the water. He sat at a wooden table with his laptop open and a cell phone pressed to his ear. It wasn't difficult to tell that he was yelling at someone, but the soundproofing on the room was top notch.

Travis saw our movement and looked up from his computer screen, signaling for us to go ahead and come inside. Savage opened the door for me and I went in, unsure how we were going to handle this from here on out. Because I knew no matter what lies we'd been telling, I wasn't going to be anyone's pirate wench this afternoon.

I didn't notice the TV screens mounted in each corner of the room until Savage had come in behind me and effectively cut off any means of escape. I made an inhuman sound in the back of my throat and wondered if there would ever be anything more awkward than this particular moment. And that was saying something, because I'd had a lot of awkward moments over the years.

Every one of the screens was showing the filming that was happening below deck.

It was like a car wreck. I couldn't look away. But I also couldn't look at Travis Elias either, because I'm not comfortable watching porn with men I've never met.

I could feel Savage's chest shaking with laughter behind me and I elbowed him in the gut. This whole thing was his fault. Or maybe it was my fault, because I'd had the bright idea to keep Rosemarie out of prison. But I felt better blaming him. The only saving grace about the whole situation was that the sound was turned off.

"Sorry to keep you two waiting," Travis said, hanging up his phone and tossing it on the table. "You the new talent?"

"Sorry to disappoint you, but no. I'm Agent Savage with the FBI. This is Addison Holmes."

"Uh huh," he said. "Nice act. But we're shooting a period piece here. Can you say Arrrgh?" He did a double take when he looked at me and said, "You look kind of familiar. Have we met before?"

"No. Most definitely not."

"It'll come to me. I never forget a face. Well, take off your clothes and let me see what I have to work with."

"I'm going to pass," Savage said, moving his badge a little closer so Travis could inspect it. "We'd like to talk to you about the murder of Priscilla Loveshack."

"You're the Feds? For real? That fucker Tim is supposed to be guarding the boat, and he just lets the FBI walk on and roam around. For fuck's sake. He's fired."

"To be fair, he does wear an eye patch," I said. "Maybe it was just hard to tell when he looked at us. And I guess Agent Savage makes a pretty convincing porn star. Unemployment is pretty high around here. Maybe Tim should keep his job."

Savage was looking at me like I'd grown a second head, so I pressed my lips together and smiled.

"Let's talk about blackmail," Savage said.

One of the coolest things I'd learned by watching law enforcement and their interrogation techniques was that most people would hang themselves with their own rope if given the chance. Travis was no exception to that rule.

"That fucking bitch. I did not know that girl was under eighteen. She wanted to be an actress. I was just giving her a chance to succeed. And there was Priscilla, taping the whole fucking thing. The right amount of money buys a lot of silence, so the girl wasn't the problem. But Priscilla was determined to take me for every last penny I had until she'd gotten enough to retire from the business and open that damn shop of hers. Not like it was anything to write home about. Everybody buys their dildos online nowadays anyway.

"So she tapped out everyone she could get her nasty little claws into until she had enough money squirreled away to go out on her own. Luckily her husband isn't the same caliber of asshole as she was, so he kept his fingers in the business that made them both stars. Some people have no loyalty. You know what I'm saying?"

It wasn't a bad afternoon's work as far as putting the puzzle together of who killed Priscilla Loveshack. If Detective Jacoby had done even a fraction of the work we had, he'd probably already have the real killer in custody.

Savage drove to Nick's house to pick up the dogs, and we waited for several minutes for Rosemarie and the dogs to have a proper reunion.

"That's just not right," my mother said. "I've never understood people who let dogs lick them right in the mouth. All dogs do is lick their buttholes, other dog's buttholes, or toilet water. You might as well eat a steaming pile of poop and call it a day."

Savage smiled tightly and I pressed my finger against my twitching eyelid. We loaded the dogs in the back and then headed down to Whiskey Bayou to drop my mother and Rosemarie off. Thank you, Jesus. It was pitch dark outside, my temples were throbbing, and I needed a bottle of wine. I looked at Savage closely and figured he was probably feeling much the same way.

"I must have it bad," Savage said. "I can't imagine any other reason for the day I just had. And if I ever have to do it again I think I'll just eat a bullet and be done with it. My eyes need bleach and my ears need cotton."

"I have those days too. But you held up well. Especially when they started asking you all those personal questions. You have a talent for giving answers without actually saying anything."

"I'm FBI, babe. That's my specialty. Did you know your eye is twitching?"

"Yep. For almost three hours now. I've been timing it.

The record is six, so I'm thinking now that there's some distance between us and them it'll go away."

"Families are supposed to make you feel that way. There's a reason I moved a thousand miles away from mine."

"I've been considering it. I'm thinking Hawaii. Or maybe Iceland. I've never been there before."

We returned to Nick's in mostly comfortable silence. The lights were on in the house, and I was surprised to see Nick's SUV parked in the driveway. It was the first night he'd been home at a regular time all week.

"It's a cool house."

We could see straight through the windows from the front of the house to the backyard, where the pool lights illuminated the water and reflected off the icy drizzle as it fell. The front door opened and Nick came out to stand on the porch—barefoot and in nothing but jeans and a white undershirt—as if it weren't freezing outside. He held a bottle of beer in his hand and his face was unreadable.

A prickle of unease went down my spine as he and Savage locked glances, and I hurried to gather my stuff.

"Thanks for the ride and the help," I said, pushing open the car door. Icy wind hit me in the face and I scooted out of the truck as gracefully as my knee would allow. "I'd say it was fun and we should do it again, but I'm with you—I'd rather eat a bullet than go through that again. You're a good sport, Savage. Even though your middle name is Earl."

He grinned and grimaced at the same time. "I had no idea Rosemarie would guess it on the first try like that. Took me off guard."

"She says she's psychic."

"You could add two letters to that word and it has a whole other meaning."

I laughed and slammed the car door shut and Savage gave a two-finger salute before driving away. I was taking my time getting up to the porch, my limp more pronounced than it had been all day, and I hadn't quite gotten the courage to look at Nick. But when I got to the porch it turned out I didn't need any courage after all. He'd already gone back inside and left me there alone.

CHAPTER FIFTEEN

THURSDAY

To say that things were awkward between me and Nick would be an understatement of epic proportions. I couldn't exactly pinpoint where things had started to go wrong, somewhere between lamp breaking sex the other morning and last night, but the churning in my gut told me it had a lot to do with Savage coming back to town.

Nick woke early and headed straight into the shower without so much as a grunt of acknowledgment, so I got up and padded downstairs to put on coffee. The swelling in my knee had gone down quite a bit, and I could mostly walk on it without limping. I was also feeling a little more in control of my emotions, so I figured that if I could get the squishy feeling to leave my stomach over whatever was bothering Nick then it would probably shape up to be a pretty good day.

I put on the coffee and then started taking out things to make pancakes. My mother had always said that the way to get a man to see reason was to feed him. But considering what a terrible cook she was, that only proved to me how much my dad really did love my mother. Because he ate every blessed meal she ever put in front of his face.

I heard Nick's footsteps padding around upstairs as I turned on the griddle. I'd watched him get dressed enough in the mornings to know his routine—undershirt, socks, and underwear from the top drawer. Then dress shirt from the closet, buttoned all the way up. Trousers pulled on and zipped. Utility belt and duty rig next. And then right before he left the bedroom he grabbed a tie from the closet and left it loose around his neck. Every time I saw that tie I lost my mind and wanted to tackle him to the floor so I could have my wicked way with him.

I looked at the clock on the microwave and frowned. He was taking longer than normal and I didn't hear him moving around anymore. He was avoiding me, which meant he was really pissed. And I wasn't going to stand for it. We were going to get to the root of the problem, if I had to lay down in the middle of the driveway to keep him from leaving for work.

I turned off the griddle and headed back toward the stairs, but Nick was already halfway down them. He took the last couple at once and skidded to a stop in his socked feet. I'd never seen him look like this—his face dark with anger and his eyes cold as ice chips.

I stopped in my tracks and gripped the back of the sofa for support. "What's wrong? What happened?"

And then I saw it. The white plastic applicator he held in his hand.

"What the hell is this? It's positive. Are you pregnant? Jesus, Addison."

A couple of months back Kate had thought she might be pregnant, so in a show of solidarity I'd picked up two pregnancy tests and taken one with her so she wouldn't have to do it alone.

We peed on the strips and then put them back in the brown paper bag they'd come in because neither of us had had the courage to look, and we decided maybe drinking a margarita or two first was the best way to build up that courage.

Kate had taken the paper bag back home with her and she said she'd call me when she was ready to see the results. I'd honestly forgotten about the whole darned thing until she'd called and flipped my entire life upside down.

"I've got good news and bad news," she'd said. "Which do you want first?"

"The good news."

"I'm not pregnant. I got my period this morning and my test was negative when I looked in the bag. I think the stress of the job is messing with my hormones."

"That's the good news?"

"I think so. I talked it over with Mike and we're going to wait another year or so before starting a family. This was a timely event. We'll be a little more careful with the birth control from now on."

"So what's the bad news?" I asked.

"Your test was positive."

I can't even describe how I'd felt as that little bomb was dropped in my lap. Terror was the first thought. I didn't know anything about being a mother. I didn't know how to grow a small person inside my body and then make sure they survived once they got out. I didn't even have a pet.

My second feeling was embarrassment, because I lived in a small town in the south. And pregnant unmarried women were still whispered about like they were the devil's candy, hell-bent on enticing all the men they encountered with their wicked ways.

My third thought was the most confusing. Somewhere deep inside of me was excitement. I don't know if it was because I'm past thirty and it turned out my ovaries weren't dried up like prunes after all, or just because I'm a woman and there's some sense of accomplishment and thrill at the idea of being able to carry another human inside you. But that excitement had been there no matter how hard I'd tried to quash it.

Those feelings were short-lived, however. It turns out buying pregnancy tests out of the bargain bin isn't always the best idea. I had no idea they could expire and give false results. But that's just what had happened.

I'm not sure why I'd kept the test, but I'd tossed the paper bag onto the corner shelf of the closet and forgot it had existed.

My mouth went dry as Nick stared me down, waiting for an answer, and I licked my lips and decided to handle this the way I normally handle things. With a false sense of bravado and defensiveness.

"I beg your pardon?" I asked, brow raised. "I don't appreciate being spoken to that way." The angrier I got, the thicker the Georgia in my voice became. I was pretty damned angry. And holy cow, did I sound like my mother.

I'd once heard a woman describe Nick Dempsey as being sexy enough to make her lady parts regenerate even though she'd had a full hysterectomy. I could sympathize. I had all my lady parts intact and every time Nick walked by I felt my ovaries clench with anticipation. My ovaries had gotten me into a lot of trouble lately.

"I asked you a question," he said. "What the hell is

this?" He held the white plastic stick as if it were a grenade instead of a pregnancy test.

Sweat beaded on his brow and his white, button-down shirt sat askew on his broad shoulders. His hair was mussed where he'd run his fingers through it repeatedly. I was only slightly concerned about the pallor of his skin.

My eyes narrowed and I wouldn't have been surprised if steam escaped my ears like the whistle on a steam engine. So maybe he'd been taken a little off guard by finding the test hidden in a paper bag and shoved in the corner of the closet. What the hell was he doing snooping through my stuff anyway?

"Were you going to show me this, or were you going to keep it a secret for the next nine months?"

"If I was going to show you I wouldn't have hidden it in the closet," I yelled. I refrained from rolling my eyes. But just barely.

The green tinge in his face disappeared and red flushed his cheeks. The little vein in his forehead bulged out and I took a step backward. I recognized the look. I was either about to get yelled at or have the best sex of my life. But because of my excellent proficiency in context clues, I was betting it wasn't the latter.

I bit my bottom lip and felt tears well in my eyes. This was not good. No woman wanted to see a reaction like the one Nick currently had when faced with the possibility of bringing children into the world together. My anger was quickly elevating from steam engine mad to nuclear levels, and if I didn't get out of the house no judge could possibly hold me responsible for what might happen.

"Answer the fucking question," he said, each word slow and distinct. "Are you pregnant?"

I sucked in a deep breath and felt it burn in my lungs.

I don't even remember my hand reaching out to grab the little crystal dish on the sofa table that held potpourri. But before I knew it the dish was sailing through the air, red tinged pieces of wood and cinnamon sticks flying in all directions. It hit Nick right in the middle of the forehead with a thunk that made me cringe. His eyes glazed and then rolled into the back of his head before he toppled to the floor.

What can I say? Hormones are a bitch.

I ran upstairs and put on my standard casualwear of yoga pants and an oversized sweater. I slid my feet into my sneakers and put on a black baseball cap, and then ran back downstairs as fast as my knee would let me.

Nick groaned on the floor. "What the hell?" He rubbed his forehead and I burst into tears.

"I'm not pregnant, you big dummy. In case you haven't noticed, I've had PMS all week."

"Oh, I've noticed."

I hiccupped through another sob and turned on my heel and headed out the door. I didn't even stop to put on my coat. I just grabbed it and my purse and ran to the car. Oh, man, was I in trouble. I'd just assaulted a cop. Not that he didn't deserve it. The idiot. But still—I did feel bad about it. I didn't usually resort to violence.

I got on the phone before I could talk myself out of anything. Normally I'd call Kate in a situation like this. She was my best friend, after all. But she was at work— like I should've been—and I knew she was swamped. I knew she would've dropped everything if I'd asked her to, which was exactly why I didn't.

"Good morning, sunshine," Rosemarie warbled a little unsteadily.

I frowned into the phone and double-checked to make sure I'd dialed the right number.

"Are you all right?"

"Right as rain. I've decided to make lemonade with these prison lemons. I'm going to keep positive and be happy even if I have to draw a smile on like the Joker."

"Have you been drinking?"

"I might have poured a little vodka in my cornflakes this morning. It turns out I didn't have any lemons for my lemonade." She hiccupped once and I burst into laughter. What a sad and bizarre pair we were.

"I was thinking it might be a good morning for some retail therapy."

"Amen, sister. I can find some accessories to go with my orange jumpsuit."

"I'm headed your way now. Don't eat any more cereal."

CHAPTER SIXTEEN

"DON'T THINK that because I'm a little tipsy that I didn't notice your eyes are swollen and your nose is red as Rudolph," Rosemarie said a short time later.

We'd decided to walk up and down Broughton Street and just return the packages to the car whenever our hands got too full. It turns out both of us were able to do quite a bit of retail damage in an hour, because the circulation was getting cut off in my fingers from all the bags.

"Nick and I had a fight this morning. I'm mostly over it now. And it's not nice to bring up my swollen face. Not everyone can be a pretty crier."

"I hear ya, girl. And maybe we should stop by Elizabeth Arden so they can put some cream on your eyes and touch up your makeup. The sales girl at Chico's kept watching to see if you were going to start stuffing scarves down the front of your blouse. Speaking of blouses, you know I'd cut off my leg before I criticized anyone, but have you seen what you're wearing today?"

I grimaced and looked down at my clothes. I was wearing red and green fleece pants tucked into my Uggs and an Atlanta Braves hooded sweatshirt that had a mustard stain right down the middle due to a hotdog mishap. My hair was pulled back into a sloppy ponytail, but I had a black beanie cap pulled down low over my ears.

My mom always used to say when we were kids that we looked like we'd just rolled out of the missionary barrel. Mostly she said that to Phoebe, because she did actually get a lot of her clothes from the lost and found at church. I was just glad my mother couldn't see me now. I'd never hear the end of it.

"It was a bad fight." I sighed and adjusted my bags as we made our way through sidewalk traffic back to the car. "I don't know what's going on. We've been having some problems, but I can't really pinpoint the reason. Other than his job is stressful and it stresses me out to know how much he hates my job."

"The way I see it, it's not stress that's the problem. The problem is that you've got one too many fish in your frying pan. Nick is threatened by Savage. He'll never come out and say so, because that wouldn't be manly. And we all know men are idiots when it comes to just saying what they really feel. What you've gotta do is reassure Nick that Savage is nothing more than a friend. He needs to know you're committed a hundred percent."

The thing about Rosemarie was that I was used to her being a train wreck, so it always took me a little off guard when she opened her mouth and good advice came out.

"Maybe you're right." I'd already made my choice. Nick was the one I loved, and Savage had just momentarily clouded my judgment.

"There's no maybe about it. A woman staring down her last days of freedom doesn't lie."

"Good point."

We were at the corner of Broughton and Abercorn, waiting for the signal to walk when a black Tahoe swerved in front of us and the doors opened. At first I thought it was a police unit, but then the sight of men holding guns on us penetrated the fog in my brain and I realized we might be in trouble.

I barely had time to blink before a man tossed me into the Tahoe. All the seats had been removed, I guess because it made it more convenient to abduct people. I kicked out with my legs and did every self-defense move I'd ever been taught, but sometimes the bad guys are just stronger.

I heard a couple of grunts and a stream of invective from Rosemarie as two guys tried to get her into the van. It would've almost been comical except for the fact that I was probably going to die. My hands were jerked together and tied with zip ties, and a bag was pulled down over my head.

I felt the Tahoe dip and heard a grunt as Rosemarie was tossed in and then we were speeding off through traffic. It seemed like we'd been there forever—surely long enough for someone to get a license plate number and call it in. But in reality, it had only taken seconds for us to be abducted.

The ties around my wrists bit into my skin and I was starting to hyperventilate from the bag over my head. Nothing in my P.I. exam had prepared me for this, and I was seriously thinking about filing a complaint about this lapse if I managed to get out of this mess.

I curled up in a little ball in the corner, my head

knocking against the door every time we hit a bump. I couldn't tell how closely I was being watched because of the bag over my head, but from the ruckus Rosemarie was making I was betting their attention was focused on her.

I stuck my hands into the front pocket of my hoodie and felt around for my phone. I knew that when the keypad came up for me to type in my code and unlock the phone that there was a button that said emergency at the bottom of the screen.

I shook my head and tried to duck my chin so I could see something other than blackness, and a nervous giggle almost escaped me when light hit my eyes. My palms were sweaty and the phone slick in my grasp, but I hit the emergency button and then just prayed.

We hit another bump and the phone shot out of my hand and down into the side pocket in the door. I was too scared to speak all the curse words I was thinking out loud, but they were bad ones, and I was probably going to have to say a prayer or two to make restitution. Though probably God would be pretty lenient, considering I'd been kidnapped and tossed like a sack of potatoes into the back of a Tahoe.

We hadn't gone too far by the time the car jerked to a stop, and my head whacked against the side of the door again.

"I'm not getting the feisty one again," one of the men said. "She kicked me right in the balls."

"You'd have to have balls for her to actually reach them," someone else said. "Don't be such a pussy."

The car doors opened and I almost rolled onto the ground. One of them grabbed me under the armpits, hauled me up, and tossed me over his shoulder. I kept my fingers crossed they wouldn't see the phone in the side panel. The bag slipped off my head and I blinked rapidly at the sudden light. My stomach was roiling from the upside-down motion, and I figured whoever was carrying me deserved a little vomit on his shoes if he kept jostling me around. I shuddered to think how they were transporting Rosemarie. She wasn't exactly easy to toss over the shoulder.

Sleet stung my face and then we were indoors and a blast of intense heat took the place of the cold. It was too hot and droplets of water dripped down my nose and plopped onto the floor.

"I'm gonna be sick," I said. It was enough to get my captor to drop me. I landed hard on my knees, and I screamed as my already abused knee took another hit. At the same time, I was grateful they'd tied my hands in front of me so I didn't smash my face against the floor. A broken nose would be very unflattering.

"Get up, bitch," he said, and pulled my hair to get me to my feet.

I caught my reflection in the metal of a set of elevator doors and recognized the look of wild-eyed panic. Tears leaked from the corners of my eyes and my breath was coming much too quickly. I caught sight of Rosemarie and saw she wasn't faring much better. Her face was pale and her eye makeup was smeared under her eyes. And if I wasn't mistaken, a bruise was forming on her cheek.

"Are you okay?" I asked her.

"I'm fine," she said as they shoved us into the elevator. "But I got a rip in my favorite pants and I don't think my bladder is as strong as it once was."

The two guys guarding Rosemarie scrunched up their faces and took a step away from her.

"I assume there's a reason you abducted two unsuspecting women right off the street."

I wasn't sure where in the city we were. It was hard to recognize landmarks when you were hanging upside-down. The building was old and the elevator rattled as we made our way to the top. From what Savage had told me about Travis Elias, I was willing to bet this was another one of his buildings used for filming.

The elevator rattled to a stop and we all balanced our weight as it gave an extra jerk at the end. The doors opened to reveal a room that didn't match the rest of the building. Everything was pure opulence—marble floors and high ceilings, plush white couches and subtle touches of art. I wondered briefly how they kept the white couches clean.

The guy assigned to me poked me in the back with his gun to push me forward and I stumbled out unsteadily.

"Lord, that's a lot of white. How do they keep it clean?" Rosemarie asked. "I had a white couch once and by the time I got rid of the thing it was so gray it looked like a thundercloud."

"Do you ever shut up, lady?" one of the men asked.

"No. And I talk a lot when I'm nervous, so you should probably prepare yourselves. 'Cause I'm pretty nervous right now with that gun pointed at me. Maybe you could put it down."

"Or maybe I'll just shoot you in the damned throat and be done with it."

"Well that would certainly make it difficult to keep the room clean. Blood isn't easy to get out of fabric."

"I want a fucking raise," the guy mumbled.

They led us down a long hallway to one of the rooms

and I had a brief moment of panic when I saw the giant white bed that was the focal point of the space. I had an even bigger moment of panic when I saw Travis Elias's body sprawled on the floor, his face bashed in to the point of almost being unrecognizable. Little black spots danced in front of my vision and I gripped the closest arm to steady my balance. My skin was cold and clammy with sweat.

The sound of gagging came from my left and when I turned to look Rosemarie slapped her hand over her mouth and squinched her eyes closed.

"Just look the other way," I told her. "If you throw up then I'll be right behind you."

She gagged one more time and then turned the other direction. "I swear, Addison. This is almost getting ridiculous. If you keep finding bodies like this I don't know if we can hang out. It's like you have a cloud of death hanging over you all the time. Like the Grim Reaper."

"Excuse me?" I asked. I'd had enough of the death references. I was not in the mood. I'd had a fight with Nick, was dressed like a rag picker, and I was having my period. "None of this is my fault. You're the one who burned the stupid motor out of your stupid vibrator. You're the one who got us into this mess by losing your damned mind and breaking shit at Priscilla's Love Shack. I just wanted to eat my scone in peace. You've got to get ahold of yourself, woman. You need sex rehab. Or more fucking donuts."

"Umm, ladies—" one of the guys tried to interrupt. But I shot him a look and he backed up a step.

"I don't need sex rehab," Rosemarie said, her voice

going shrill. "What I need is the product I paid for to work. And it's not like I knew we were going to find a dead body. But I shoulda figured, with you along for the ride. Which reminds me, I'm going to give that Detective Jacoby a piece of my mind the next time I see him. I'm a tax paying citizen. I got rights. And he stole my motherfucking M&Ms. Who does shit like that?"

"Ladies—" the guy said again.

"Can't you see we're in the middle of something?" I said. I ignored him and then turned back to Rosemarie. "I'm just saying that I think you owe me an apology for the death comment. What's a few bodies here and there? Look at all the people I encounter on a daily basis who are still alive."

Rosemarie nodded sagely. "That's a good point. I didn't consider that aspect. I apologize for associating the cloud of death with your name."

"If you ladies are finished with your campfire confessions we can get down to business."

I recognized that voice, and I guess I shouldn't have been too surprised to see him here. With Travis Elias dead, there was really only one other who benefitted the most from Priscilla's death.

I hadn't liked Lance Mayhew the first time I'd met him. There's got to be a special place in hell for that kind of narcissism, and even now he was posed against the doorframe, one foot crossed in front of the other, his long flowing locks hanging over one shoulder. His shirt was unbuttoned down to the middle of his chest and his slacks were crisply pressed.

"You look just like the guy on that fake butter commercial, except you're a little thicker around the waist." Rosemarie said. "Makes me hungry."

Anger flashed across Lance's face and he stood up straight, crossing his arms over his chest. Apparently he didn't like hearing he was thick around the waist. He also didn't have good control over his emotions, which could be bad for our continued health. Anyone with a quick trigger finger had to be handled delicately. And neither of us were known for our subtlety.

"I'll make this fast, because I don't particularly care to draw this out or prolong your lives in any way." He looked at Rosemarie and she audibly gulped and grabbed my hand. "My wife gave you something when you visited her store. I want it back. And if you think to hold out on me because I'm going to kill you anyway, then know that I have no problem torturing you until someone gives me the information I want. Big Brutus over there has a taste for the zaftig ladies."

Rosemarie and I both turned our heads in unison and stared at Big Brutus. He was built like a bull and kind of looked like one too. He smiled and rubbed the front of his crotch until it looked like he had a baseball bat stuffed down the front of his pants.

I didn't want to say it, but I was sure glad Big Brutus liked zaftig women.

"Don't get me wrong," Rosemarie said. "That's a pretty intimidating threat, and I'm going to take it under consideration once you tell me what the hell Priscilla supposedly gave to me. But I think what I'm most surprised about right now is that you know what zaftig means and used it correctly in a sentence. I don't want to offend you or anything, but you don't seem all that bright."

"Neither do you. Most people wouldn't be mouthing off in front of someone pointing a gun at them."

Rosemarie shrugged like it was a common occurrence to be held at gunpoint, and I decided at that point to let her do the talking.

"You said you were going to kill us anyway. What have we got to lose?"

I wasn't too sure I was all that fond of Rosemarie's use of the collective we. I was still trying to figure out how I'd gotten lumped into this mess. If only I'd called Kate to go shopping instead of Rosemarie, my future would be looking quite a bit brighter right now.

I tried to be as covert as possible in scanning the room. There were the four guys who'd kidnapped us at our back, plus two more that had appeared once we'd gotten to the top floor. It was all a little blurry after I saw Travis Elias's body. I didn't see Pirate Pete anywhere, so I was assuming Travis had made good on his threat and fired him. Which was kind of a shame. He seemed like an affable enough guy.

"Just hand over the thumb drive and I'll make sure it's a quick death. It's the best I can do under the circumstances."

"I'm telling you, I don't know anything about a thumb drive or anything else your wide supposedly gave me. The only thing that woman gave me was a busted vibrator."

Rosemarie dug around in her cross body bag and whipped out the vibrator, much the same as she had a few days before. The guy standing closest to her dodged in the nick of time. If that thing had made contact with his face, he would've been down for the count. It definitely had some heft behind it. I could only imagine that Rosemarie's vaginal muscles must be like one of those walnut crunchers to take down such a mighty beast. It made what happened to Leroy all the more scary.

I shook my head in wonder as a room full of men looked around, unsure of what course of action to take when a crazed woman was swinging a dildo.

"I barely got a handful of uses out of it before it petered out. So I took it back to the store and she shipped it back to the manufacturer. But when it came back it was the same thing all over again. It'd barely get going before it died, dead as a doornail. So I took it back again on Monday night and she was real rude this time. Like it was my fault or something."

"She was a bitch on wheels," Lance said. "But she was fucking brilliant." He got a funny look on his face when he stared at the vibrator and then he said, "Open it up like you're going to take the batteries out."

"This is the plug-in model," Rosemarie said. "It revs like a damned lawnmower."

"It's the newest model. They have a battery backup just in case you need to travel and are unable to find an outlet."

"Huh. I didn't know that. That's real convenient if you're camping in the woods or something."

"Jesus," I said, shaking my head. "Let me see the damned thing. I'm ready for them to put bullets in our heads already."

"You can be a real bitch when you're on your period," she huffed, handing over the vibrator.

I gave her my best bitch look and took the device between the tips of my fingers. "What's the big deal about finding a stupid flash drive anyway?" I asked. "Priscilla's dead. It's not like anyone needs to know she had it."

"Just because she's dead doesn't mean it couldn't end up in the wrong hands. There's a lot of sensitive information on the drive. How the hell do you think she knew who to squeeze for money? After she'd gotten enough money to retire from the industry and open that shop of hers she was supposed to stop with the blackmail. But she loved the money too much. And mostly she just liked wringing the life out of the people she despised. She was a vicious, vengeful bitch."

"You should have a care about how you speak of the dead," Rosemarie said. "What kind of manners is that?"

"Was she squeezing you for money too?" I asked, trying to divert his attention back to me in case he was tempted to put a bullet in Rosemarie's brain prematurely.

"No, but I was business partners with Travis and a few other guys on the list. As soon as she started her demands for more money, who do you think they started taking it out on? They cut me out of a real estate deal I'd sunk millions into and they were getting ready to cut me off permanently."

I unscrewed the bottom of the device and there was a plastic tab covering the place reserved for the batteries. I worked at it with my thumbnail until it popped right off. And sure enough, inside was a silver flash drive in place of the batteries.

Sweat snaked down my spine, because I knew the moment they had that flash drive in their hands they'd shoot us. And despite my flippant statement a little earlier, I really wasn't ready to die.

Almost as if my prayers were being answered, all of the lights in the room turned off and there was a few precious seconds of surprised silence before all hell broke loose. I had enough wherewithal to launch myself at Rosemarie and take us both to the floor before bullets started flying.

I choked back a scream as one flew so close to my

head that I could feel the heat against my scalp. This was another scenario that hadn't been covered in my P.I. training. I was starting to think that maybe I hadn't gotten my money's worth.

My ears rang and my nostrils burned from the acrid smell of gunfire. Then as quick as they'd gone off, the lights all turned back on again in a blinding rush, and hands were pulling me from Rosemarie's grasp. I was too weak to fight them off, and I hoped it was the good guys who'd won once the smoke had cleared.

"Addison," Nick said, but it sounded like he was far away. I blinked my eyes several times and waited for them to adjust until he came into focus. "Are you all right?"

I read his lips this time, because my ears were still ringing something awful. "I'm fine," I said. "Thanks for rescuing us."

"Smart move leaving the phone on. Dispatch got it all and was able to trace your location. Added that to all the phone calls we got as soon as you were abducted, and it didn't take long to mobilize and track you down."

"I just wanted to say I'm sorry about this morning. I think I might have overreacted." I couldn't tell how loud I was talking, but by the way Nick flinched every time I said a word I was guessing it was pretty loud. Not to mention, most of the other cops had stopped what they were doing to listen in on the conversation. "How's your head?"

"It's still attached to my neck. I don't mean to change the subject, but I don't remember your hair being that short on the left this morning before you addled my brains."

I gasped and reached up to touch the side of my head and sure enough, the hair there was only a couple of inches long. A sob caught in my throat and I kept tugging at the hair, hoping I could somehow make it grow longer in an instant.

"They shot my hair off," I said pathetically.

"Look on the bright side. It could've been your face."

EPILOGUE

Friday

I meant to go into the agency first thing, but I found myself driving the streets of Savannah, watching joggers and bicyclists dodge each other on the sidewalk and a mugger attempt to snatch a lady's purse in front of the Walgreens. She laid him out flat with an elbow to the face, adjusted her coat, and kept walking like nothing had ever happened.

I'm not sure what propelled me toward the little house Phoebe had just vacated, but the car headed in that direction of its own free will. I took the key from under the mat and let myself inside. I didn't worry about Spock, Savage, or the other neighbors who might be watching my every move. I just needed to clear my head in a quiet space and think over my options.

Nick's reaction to the pregnancy test still smarted. I guess I thought if he was committed enough for us to live together then he'd man up enough to stay committed if that pregnancy test had been accurate.

I heard a car door slam from the street, but didn't give

it much thought. It was a busy street and people were always coming and going. But I was surprised to hear the knock on the door and see Nick stick his head inside.

"Can I come in?" he asked. His voice was morning deep and stubble was thick on his cheeks. His eyes were tired and a little wary, but I still felt my heart flutter at the sight of him.

"Sure," I said.

"What are you doing here?"

"I just thought I'd come and look around. How did you know where to find me?"

"I know you well. And I wanted to say something before you think about moving out and coming back to live here."

I opened my mouth to deny it, but I realized maybe that was the reason I'd stopped by. Nick did know me well.

"It's possible I didn't handle the pregnancy test incident in the best possible way."

I arched a brow and crossed my arms under my breasts. "You think?"

"It took me off guard. And I was pissed you decided to hide it from me, if you want to know the truth." He shrugged and I could tell he was uncomfortable with this conversation. Nick wasn't exactly known for sharing his feelings. Come to think of it, I was starting to think it was a trait all cops shared.

I sighed and dropped my arms down to my sides. "Maybe I overreacted a little too. I'm sorry about your head."

The corner of his mouth kicked up in a smile and he moved a little closer. "It's taken worse knocks." He kept coming until he stood directly in front of me, his body barely touching mine, but enough for me to feel the heat. And then he kissed me and I felt the stress and worry and pain of the week disappear.

I could've kissed for hours. Days. Nick was a premium kisser. And when he pulled away I might have grasped on a little desperately to his shoulders and tried to pull him back.

"I just wanted to say that I wasn't myself this week. I had something important on my mind, and it kept growing until it was almost consuming. So just hear me out, okay?"

He was looking a little sick all of a sudden and I was starting to get worried. What if he had a disease or something, and was trying to find the best way to tell me he only had six months to live?

He reached into his jacket pocket and pulled out a black velvet box, and black spots danced in front of my eyes. My lungs constricted and I realized I wasn't breathing, so I sucked in a deep breath and stumbled back a step. Nick steadied me by grabbing onto my hands and then he did the unthinkable.

He knelt down in front of me.

"Holy shit. What are you doing?"

Nick barked out a laugh and shook his head, squeezing my hand once before releasing it. "Only you would say that at a time like this."

"I'll be quiet."

"That would probably be best. So what do you say, Addison Holmes? Will you marry me?"

My throat closed up and I felt the edge of panic licking across my skin. If I'd been given the choice of picking any scenario that might happen on a Friday morning after I'd been kidnapped and roughed up, it never would've been this one.

I opened my mouth, hoping the right words would come out, but I was saved by the bell when there was a knock at the door.

Nick and I both turned to see Savage standing on the other side of the screen door.

"Am I interrupting anything?"

ABOUT THE AUTHOR

Liliana Hart is a *New York Times, USA Today, and Publisher's Weekly* Bestselling Author of more than 50 titles. After starting her first novel her freshman year of college, she immediately became addicted to writing and knew she'd found what she was meant to do with her life. She has no idea why she majored in music.

Liliana can almost always be found at her computer writing, hauling five kids to activities, or traveling with her husband. They call Texas home.

If you enjoyed reading *Whiskey Sour*, I would appreciate it if you would help others enjoy this book, too.

Lend it. This e-book is lending-enabled, so please, share it with a friend.

Recommend it. Please help other readers find this

book by recommending it to friends, readers' groups and discussion boards.

Review it. Please tell other readers why you liked this book by reviewing. If you do write a review, please send me an email at lilianahartauthor@gmail.com so I can thank you with a personal email. Or visit me at http://www.lilianahart.com.

Connect with me online:
www.lilianahart.com

1001 Dark Nights: Captured in Surrender

1001 Dark Nights: The Promise of Surrender

Sweet Surrender

Dawn of Surrender

The MacKenzie World (read in any order)

Trouble Maker

Bullet Proof

Deep Trouble

Delta Rescue

Desire and Ice

Rush

Spies and Stilettos

Wicked Hot

Hot Witness

Avenged

Never Surrender

JJ Graves Mystery Series

Dirty Little Secrets

A Dirty Shame

Dirty Rotten Scoundrel

Down and Dirty

Dirty Deeds

Dirty Laundry

Dirty Money

Addison Holmes Mystery Series

Whiskey Rebellion

Whiskey Sour

Whiskey For Breakfast

Whiskey, You're The Devil

Whiskey on the Rocks

Whiskey Tango Foxtrot

Whiskey and Gunpowder

The Gravediggers

The Darkest Corner

Gone to Dust

Say No More

Stand Alone Titles

Breath of Fire

Kill Shot

Catch Me If You Can

All About Eve

Paradise Disguised

Island Home

The Witching Hour

Books by Liliana Hart and Scott Silverii
The Harley and Davidson Mystery Series

The Farmer's Slaughter

A Tisket a Casket

I Saw Mommy Killing Santa Claus

Get Your Murder Running

Deceased and Desist